Saleha Chowdhury

Collected Short Stories

Collected Short Stories

By Saleha Chowdhury

Copyright©2022 by Saleha Chowdhury

First Published in May 2022

Jacket Design : Ayub Al-Amin

ISBN : 9798817172843

Contents

1 Abul Ishaq and the Bird of Dawn 7

2 The Spider 21

3 A Punk and Gulshan Ara 35

4 A Stopwatch and 400 Calories 41

5 Desdemona's Handkerchief 59

6 A Sumptuous Lunch 79

7 A Pretty Woman in an Office 91

8 Rahim and Karim 103

9 Father and They 116

10 One Kilogram of Holy Meat 128

11 Proteins, Minerals, Nigela Seeds 141

12 The Disappearance of Gopal Maker 162

13 Moses 177

14 Mr. Brown's Feeling of Loeliness 193

15 Two Lovers of Alisha And One More 205

16 Mira Sayal's Rose Garden 228

17 Talking Their Hearts Out 251

Acknowledgement

I am grateful to the translators whose contributions have made this book a reality. Niaz Zaman edited the book and I am indebted to her too. Uday Shankar Durjay does help me for a long time in different areas of my everyday life. I call him 'My God Send.' Without his help the book would never be a printed one and stay as a manuscript in my word document.

I am grateful to Rachel Webster for her lovely note of introduction. Some people's kindness make us tearful and one fine morning, after reading some of my stories, Rachel's unexpected email made me that too - tearful.

Ayub Alamin emailed me the cover with huge good wishes and I feel lucky for his contribution too. My heartfelt thanks to him.

I hope readers would read the book not with sharp criticism but with love and empathy. As you all know English is my second language. If any reader finds a better word and grammar to replace one or two of mine, please, I just politely say I learn this multifoliate English language everyday and never dreamt of telling my readers 'I am perfect.' If you enjoy the book, I would say I get more than my fair share of happiness. Thanks for reading.

Saleha Chowdhury
London May 2022

For

Four friends from my University days through thick
and thin And Sick and sin
Ferdousi Mojumdar
Ramendu Mojumdar
Denis Dilip Dutta
Aminul Islam Bedu

Cheers!

Abul Ishaq and the Bird of Dawn

Even slapping his wife gave Abul Ishaq no satisfaction. This was the first time in their marriage that he had laid hands on his wife. The first time in seven years. What was the reason? Was it because she had fallen in love with someone else or because she had slept with someone else? No. The reason was far more serious. While putting clothes in the washing machine, Zarina had washed away Abul Ishaq's quarter million pounds. How? That day, as was usual, Abul Ishaq had bought a lottery ticket and put it in the pocket of his trousers. Normally, he would take it out later and put the ticket in the drawer of the small table. For the past ten years or so he had been buying a lottery ticket with the same number. 10 17 21 25 40 50. His birthday was on the tenth. Zarina's was on the seventeenth. They were married on the twenty-first. Zarina was now twenty-five. He himself was thirty-six but he believed that before he was forty he would win the lottery. He had started with these numbers at the age of thirty. Now he was close to forty. He thought he would win the lottery now, and when he was fifty they would have no financial worries.

A palmist had told him, "There is a possibility of your coming into some money when you are forty."

The man had also said, "My prediction will be correct. At that age, you will get

a lot of money and with that you will live comfortably for the rest of your life. "

Two hundred and fifty thousand pounds would ensure a comfortable life. He would buy a house with one hundred and fifty thousand pounds. A beautiful small house with two rooms. He had seen the house when he and Zarina went for a walk. There was a "Sale" sign on the house. It was at the end of Honeysuckle Lane. It was a semi-detached house. It would take him hardly a month to transform the place into an awesome house. He knew his friend Raqibul would help him. With their sweat they would increase the value of the house to three hundred thousand pounds or even more.

He would put the rest of the money in the bank and earn interest. Or he might start some business. He would be both proprietor and worker. His planning was all right. The palmist's prophecy had also come true. If only Zarina had removed the lottery ticket from the pocket of his trousers before putting his trousers in the washing machine, everything would have been all right. True, the fault was not Zarina's . Ishaq would always keep the lottery ticket inside the *Wazifa Sharif*, the book of *doas*. After purchasing the lottery ticket from the shop, he would put it inside his pocket of his trousers. From there he would transfer it to the *Wazifa Sharif,* was kept in a special drawer, along with the *attars, tasbih,* and the carnelian stone.

Abul Ishaq was a fairly pious Muslim, saying the prescribed prayers, keeping the obligatory fasts. He worked hard all year long. He worked in a shop, selling goods, keeping the accounts, bringing down heavy stuff from lorries. He and his wife were able to manage with what the owner paid him. Zarina did not work. Abul Ishaq would say to her, "What is the need for you to work? We have no children. It's just the two of us. We can manage with my earning."

Nor did Zarina have the education or intelligence to work in London. She had only studied up to class nine. She could perhaps have found work in some factory but Abul Ishaq would say, "It's not necessary. Stay at home."

Abul Ishaq was an only child. Both his parents had passed away. There were no relations back home to draw him there. Abul Ishaq had married Zarina for her looks. She had large eyes and a sweet, dusky complexion. The two were a fairly happy couple. Zarina's time passed in cleaning and tidying the house, cooking the food, going to the stores for groceries, saying her prayers five times a day, and keeping the fasts. And occasional going out.

Zarina had a maternal uncle in London. After Abul Ishaq slapped her, she left the house with just the clothes in a bag. Furious at her, Abul Ishaq bellowed, "Don't ever come back to this house. Miserable woman. Don't you have the sense to check pockets before putting trousers in the washing machine? "

After that Abul Ishaq had slapped Zarina hard. Then he had said, "From today the doors of this house are shut for you."

Zarina had said nothing after the slap. Hadn't she too suffered on learning what she had done? Wasn't she too feeling untold agonies at the mishap? The slap was nothing compared to what she was suffering. Still, she wept and said, "All right. I will not come back."

In order to go to her uncle's place she boarded the No 36 bus. In her small purse she had ten pounds and the house keys. She had come away with only these. Her uncle lived in a council house. It had four rooms, a kitchen and a balcony. On the balcony, her uncle grew green chillies and tomatoes. A little kitchem garden in the balcony The pain of losing the house they had seen and which they had wished to buy, the pain of losing the remaining money was much greater than if Abul Ishaq had slashed her with a knife and poured salt Into the wounds. A beautiful house of their own! Just thinking about it caused her heart to swell with agony. She would have decorated the house and grown flowers and vegetables in the garden behind. She wiped her eyes as she thought of all the things they could have done in that house.

Zarina's uncle looked at her from the corner of his eyes. "It's a man's fate to have children, it's a woman's to acquire wealth. You are not fated to have so much money. Forget what has happened. Don't rub salt into the wound. Stay here until your husband comes to his senses."

Then he said, "Alas, alas, two hundred and fifty thousand pounds. Alas." Slapping his forehead Zarina"s uncle walked away.

Tired and exhausted, Zarina stared up at the ceiling. She had always checked pockets before putting clothes in the washing machine. Why hadn't she checked the pockets that day? Burying her face in the pillow, she wept.

Abul Ishaq took seven days' leave to recover from his grief. Holidays were due . They would have gone to visit their country. They would have returned after donating some money to a mosque. After that, what a life of comfort they would have lived. Both of them would also have completed their hajj. The palmist had told him, "The lines on one's hand change. But the line showing that you will get money is so deep that I don't think that it will change." Why did it change? Why didn't he get the money? These thoughts almost drove Abul Ishaq insane. He wandered about here and there. Was it all a game? How dull everything seemed. He thought of what could have happened and what had happened instead. He looked at the lines of his hand repeatedly. He knew them by heart. The heart line, the life line, the head line, the fate line. Which of these was the money line? He was not sure. But it must be somewhere. Otherwise why would the palmist have said what he did?

At the sound of the bus, he lifted his eyes. He did not remember when he had boarded the bus and come to Trafalgar Square. He watched the pigeons flying about. He saw the crowds of people everywhere. They were engaged in different activities, walking, laughing, talking, even saying nothing at all. He thought, Surely none of them is suffering the way I am. Then he returned to his earlier thoughts. Finally, he thought he would return home. From the next day he would go to work again. It didn't seem that he had any wish to bring Zarina back. Zarina's uncle had told him, "Son, Zarina is here. Don't worry about her. She never wants to come to visit us. Now that she is here, let her remain a few days." Both Zarina's uncle and his wife worked and were fairly well off.

No, he was not worrying about Zarina. The only things on his mind were the house, a small car and money in the bank. A small business of his own.

The shopkeeper told him, "How long are you going to stay depressed like this? Put your mind in your work. Cheer up."

Abul Ishaq didn't say anything, just busied himself with his work. Someone had put his news in the papers. `The big fish had slipped out of his grasp'.

His story had been told in great detail. Several persons in London now knew his name.

Exactly a month had passed. Zarina was still in her Mama's house. In reply to Zarina's question, Mama had only said, "Stay a few days longer. He will cool down. Stay as long as you wish."

During the long hot days like big Swans eggs of July, Zarina kept two fasts every week. Her Mami went to work. The son and daughter went to university. Zarina cooked for them. They relished her cooking. That is why they were not worried about her staying. The boy came home occasionally. The girl stayed at home. Zarina too got a room to herself in the four bed-roomed house. That day Zarina was fasting. Saying her prayers on the prayer rug on the carpeted room, Zarina had fallen asleep while praying. The fragrance of frankincense enveloped her. The dimly lit room seemed to be bathed in moonlight. Zarina had no idea when, in the midst of all this, she had fallen asleep.

Suddenly she saw that her mother-in-law was sitting on one side of the bed.

Her mother-in-law greeted her. " How are you, Zari? It's so sad. My son is not eating or sleeping properly. What are you doing here? You have your own house. You have the keys. Go back immediately. Have a good wash and beg forgiveness. He is your god in this life and the next."

Zarina looked at her mother-in-law in the dim light of the room. She had passed away five years ago.

Her mother-in-law was speaking again. "Do you remember, Zari, how you had flung the rolling pin at my cat? The cat died as a result. I know that you did not mean to kill it. But the cat cursed you, Zari. Who knows how long a cat's curses last? That is why the big fish slipped out of your hands. You haven't been blessed with a child. You did not know, Zari, that my cat Tuni was pregnant at the time. Tell me what you want to do. It is not your fault."

Her mother-in-law fell silent for a while. Then she said, "It is time for me to come back to the house. How do I do that, Zari?"

Zari could say nothing. She just stared at her direction in the dim light. She wanted to say, "Ma, I didn't fling the rolling pin to kill Tuni. I had only wanted to frighten her a little. I didn't know she was expecting, Ma. Ma, Ma, how I can be released from the curse?"

While speaking, Zarina got up and sat on the bed. There was no one there. It was dark in the room. Her Mama's house was silent.

When Zarina woke up, she saw that she was alone. There was not even a shadow of her mother-in-law. Her mother-in-law had loved her like a daughter. That is why she had never addressed her as "Bou" or "Bou Ma," but always as "Zari."

Zarina said, "You have to come, Ma, in any way you can."

She saw that the darkness in the room had been lit up by moonlight.

She wondered how her mother-in-law might be able to return from the world beyond. Perhaps her mother-in-law too was thinking the same thing where she was. She whispered -"Dear Allah how that be possible!"

Tired with thinking, Zarina fell asleep.

Early next morning, before the sun had risen, Ishaq opened the door and stepped outside. He felt as if his mother was sitting close to him. Even though it was still dark, he decided to go to the meadow where he occasionally went for a walk. There was no one about. Who would be about at five in the morning? Everyone came after eight. Even those who walked their dogs didn't venture forth so early. Seeing Ishaq the trees awoke and then went back to sleep. Under a tree with large leaves was a bench on which Ishaq sat down. He didn't feel like walking. All sorts of thoughts passed through his mind as he sat there. He thought of his mother; he thought of his father. Those who were no longer in his life. Zari's face floated before his eyes. His harsh feelings had softened somewhat. Still, he thought he would not go to bring Zari back. He did not yet know when he would do so.

In front of a line of green trees, he spotted something like a white bird. From the line of trees, a path led into the deep wood. Even in the day time, the place was full of shadows. Sometimes, seabirds would come to that spot. They would fly about and then fly off into the sky. White birds, blue birds, striped birds.

Looking at the birds, Zarina would sometimes ask, "Tell me, where do those birds come from?"

Ishaq would reply, "Who knows? Perhaps from the sky. Or perhaps the sea. Remember that the sea is not far from where we are."

But the bird he was seeing now was large – like an albatross. It was slowly approaching him.

The sun had not risen. Perhaps it was about to, but its rays had not yet dispelled the mysteries of the meadow.

Ishaq was deep in thought but then he realized that the bird was no long there. The light of the morning sun lit up the park. He had never seen a field like this in Dhaka. Not even in his village home. They called it meadow in here, lovely grassy large open space.. Whenever he walked about here, he had all sorts of thoughts. Abul Ishaq was very fond of this meadow.

Ishaq had no idea when someone, all dressed in white, came and sat down beside him. The man was looking at the meadow. What a glowing face he had. His beard was totally white. For a long time he sat there quietly.

Suddenly Ishaq heard the man say, "Both your eyes . . . ."

"Both my eyes?"

"I was just saying. Both my younger brother's eyes suddenly developed a problem. He spent vast sums of money but could not get his vision back. Now he dwells in a dark world. How much money would you spend for your eyes?"

"To get my vision back?"

"Yes, something like that."

"I would sell everything I possess to get my eyes back." For some days he had not wanted to talk to anyone. Now he didn't feel bad talking to this man who resembled a bird. It seemed as if the man had emerged from a bird.

"And if one of your kidneys is damaged? My maternal uncle's daughter spent ten hundred thousand takas to get a kidney. And you know what happened? Her body rejected the kidney. That lump of flesh had to be removed and she had to go on dialysis again. Who knows how long she will live."

"Why are you telling me all these things?

"Are the things we get at no cost of no value? Kidney, heart, liver, hearing, sight, mobility, the ability to talk? If you think with a cool mind, can you calculate the value of the things Allah has given us? Teeth, eyes, nose,ears, brains – what would be the value of all these things?"

"A million million pounds. A million million pounds. Can one calculate the value of these things?" Ishaq asked.

The man asked again, "How much would you spend on being able to see?"

"Everything I have," Ishaq replied.

"Your sight, hearing, mobility, speech, taste, ability to think, the power in your hands – which of these could you give me if I gave you a million pounds?"

"I cannot give you a single one of these things. No matter how much you give me, I will not give you any one of these. These are mine. Allah has gifted me these things. I will not give you even one of these in exchange for money."

"My friend's daughter was crippled in an accident. Now she is confined to a wheelchair. She received two million pounds as compensation. She says to me, 'Chacha, if I could walk like you again, I would give the two million pounds back to them."

Ishaq was listening to the man. Thinking about all sorts of things as he did so.

Suddenly Ishaq realized that the man was no longer beside him. There was no one there. The only thing he saw was a large bird spreading its wings in the east and flying off. The bird was large, white, like an albatross.

Ishaq looked around carefully. Trees. Birds. Grass.

He got up. He took a few steps. Then he muttered to himself, "A million pounds, a million pounds." Then, with his cool brain, he started calculating the value of his strong body, his ability to work and talk. The man had said, "My brother is willing to spend two million pounds to get back his sight. He is a rich man. A million pounds is nothing for him. Can one get everything if one has money? How much did the girl in the wheelchair want to give for the ability to walk about like us?"

Ishaq looked about him. No one had come to the meadow yet. His legs were trembling strangely. He looked about him carefully. Where did the man go? Had he just imagined the man? Otherwise, where could the man have gone? After about six weeks, Ishaq could think clearly. The things he had were plenty. The things he didn't have matter? His body felt light. In the gentle breeze, he remembered the words of a song, and whistled softly. The July breeze ruffled the leaves above him, lightening his spirit. And in that meadow filled with trees and birds, Ishaq realized a lot of things anew. The pain in his heart was not bothering him as before, was not submerging him in a river of flame. Ishaq had emerged from that river. With light steps, he followed the narrow path towards his house.

"Zarina, when are you coming home?"

Zarina didn't respond for some time. Then she said, "Speak to Mami."

Mami took the telephone from her. Without any preamble she said, "Baba Dulamiah, good news. Our Zarina is expecting."

"What are you saying, Mami? How is this possible? Mami, give the phone to Zarina." He said to Zarina with excitement mixed with belief and disbelief in his voice, "Zarina! Truly?"

Mami had left the room. Zarina said, "I just learned it yesterday. My periods are irregular. But the doctor said, 'This has nothing to do with your irregular periods. You are having a baby.' "

The two were silent for some time.

Then Ishaq said, the happiness bubbling in his voice, "Zarina, Allah is truly kind. Allah has given us more than enough. And this news today! Allah is compassionate and merciful. All-forgiving. He is omnipotent. Bountiful!"

When Ishaq's excitement had died down a little, Zarina spoke in a very normal voice," I am going to name her Hasina. My mother-in-law's name. I will call her Hashi."

"How do you know that you will have a girl?"

Zarina replied calmly,"I know."

Translated by Niaz Zaman

The Spiders

Rurki Rahim and Obaidul Odud got married at last. A second marriage for both. Two years ago Rurki's husband had been killed in a car crash. For the last ten years Obaidul Odud's wife had been in a lunatic asylum, not dead yet, but insane. Obaidul Odud had seen Rurki first at a party. Poor Obaidul was wifeless and had been living alone for the last ten years. And Rurki? With her late husband's fat insurance, his share profits, his attractive bank balance, her life became very different and she looked a thousand times more glamorous than before. It was as if overnight Rurki had stepped up into a rich elite class. Perhaps, for this reason, her body and face looked very classy. She glowed like a scented candle in a dark room. But it's true that Rurki had never looked ordinary, now she looked a lot better. And though she had never belonged to an ordinary class, now everything about her revealed that she belonged to the higher class and that she was suited really well there. She had moved effortlessly from housewife to socialite. As she did not have to put up with some of her husband's bad habits anymore, ultimate independence was in her reach. Her lifestyle changed and she looked both classy and seductive. A good work-out, her beautician's hard work – all made her look like a youthful, seductive actress. Though her rise had not been unexpected, still she became the talk of the town. A bright bubbly butterfly had come out from its cocoon and had morphed from a shy caterpillar to a bright and colourful butterfly. It was as if a sabre had come out from its sheathe to take on the world. Her waist was reduced to twenty-two inches, and her busts were any woman's answer to a prayer. Her face glowed with a golden tan. And her nose, eyes, lips, neck and cheeks were well-crafted and blessed by the Great Creator. This was the situation when one day at an elite party Rurki and Obaidul met.

Obaidul Odud was an international garment merchant. Eventually he managed to get her away from the crowd and they sat cosily in a shadowy corner, drinking and talking. Obaidul Odud cleverly mentioned his yearly business turnover and she was stunned and hooked. Actually that was what she was after – money, money and more money. When Odud had first glimpsed her from behind, he wanted to know who was this Marilyn Monroe? When she turned her face, he was speechless. He did not beat around the bush but asked her straight, "Where are we going now? Your place or mine?"

They decided to go to the Five Star and spent the night there. In the morning, standing on the balcony, he proposed and she accepted. But she thought to herself, If I get bored with a garment merchant, I can always invite a poet or a violinist and can tell the world I'm not only rich but cultured too and understand the fine arts. Obaidul will be very busy with his large international business and will not have the time to watch over me all day long. Obaidul Odud had not been living a saintly life either. But his relationships with some of the women were short-lived, one-off matters or one-night stands. Some dishy women, factory workers from his factories who would do anything to please their master, a friend's sex-starved wife, and one university student who had needed money badly. All were short-lived, casual relationships. But this was the first time he seriously wanted to get married again. But he thought to himself, those dishy women workers will always be there if I need any change. So these two persons' thoughts were not very different.

Now Rurki was a bit suspicious about the insanity of Obaidul Odud's wife. She had heard a lot of rumours. People gossiped and whispered that he was the reason for her madness. The rumour was that one day he scared her with a big fat snake, knowing that she had an abnormal fear of snakes. People also said that his wife's screams could be heard for miles until madness destroyed her mind and silenced her. He claimed that it had only been a practical joke; the snake was not poisonous. Still, he was aware of his wife's snake phobia, wasn't he? So the gossip never stopped. She could kiss a tiger but a teeny-weeny snake would make her shiver and freeze, put her off-balance. Why did he do that? She heard others say that Obaidul Odud's wife would compare her husband with the intellectual professor she had had an affair with before their marriage. She called Obaidul Odud insensitive, thick-headed, boring. At one point she shouted at him, "I do not like you. You are a boring clothes merchant. You have no imagination!" So, perhaps to show his brilliance and imagination, he planned a practical joke with a real snake! He had kept it under her bed in a basket. Rurki had listened to that story over and over again. She asked him, "Why did you do that?" He replied, "It was only fun, Rurki. It had no fangs, you know."

"What did you expect from that practical joke?" Rurki asked another question to satisfy herself.

"Nothing, really. I expected she would hug me to death out of fear and would look at me as her saviour, throw her arms around me and love only me."

Rurki wanted to say, "You thick-headed maniac." But she controlled herself.

Obaidul told her, "You must never discuss that subject again."

"Never," Rurki promised.

Then his mood changed. He whispered, "Rurki, I'm so glad to meet you at last." Looking deep into her kajol- eyes, he embraced her.

"Me too, Obaidul," she said, looking at his attractive physique and thinking about his mountain of money.

Obaidul's gaze was long and deep. People said Obaidul could hypnotise women with his gaze. Women sort of surrendered willingly to his wishes. Now Rurki surrendered completely and waited for the big day. The big day came. They got married.

Rurki's friend asked her on the telephone, "What did you see in him? That sadistic moron who made his wife insane? Don't you know that story?"

Rurki replied, "An international garment merchant with billions of foreign money, a villa, an excellent physique does not grow on trees, you know. Lots of wives become mad at some point in their lives. No big deal. But this businessman's wealth! God! I told you wealth does not grow on trees."

"It grows on factory floors with the blood and sweat of unpaid or underpaid workers."

The line got cut off. Who was going to listen to all that? Jealous, shitty bitch! Rurki did not have any time for this Marxism. Then she thought, he is one in a million and he is mine.

When Rurki saw Obaidul's "Gulmohor Villa," she gaped at it, her mouth wide open. She found it hard to close her mouth again. What a huge house! About ten bedrooms, a massive swimming pool, work-out rooms, a sauna, a jacuzzi and a tennis court.

"You have to play tennis, Rurki. Do you play?"

"But I can learn."

"You have to. I like a tennis player." He winked at her.

"I see," Rurki smiled. "Only tennis?"

"All sorts of games, my dear. The seductive and sexy ones are the best."

Rurki realised the man slept on a mattress stuffed with money. All big notes. No loose change. She patted herself on her back again at her wise selection. She felt they were tailormade for each other; she had chosen well.

"Where would you like to go for a honeymoon?" Obaidul asked.

"You choose the place and surprise me."

"I will. I will take you to a place you never dreamt off. It's between Seychelles and Mauritius. A small private island. Remote, quiet and tranquil. No big hotels, no commercial casinos and juke boxes. A few chalets here and there. Cute and cosy like a green bird's nest. Lush green trees with flowers everywhere. I have been there once and understood it is a paradise."

"You know something, Obaidul? If I have to go hell with you, I would be happy."

Obaidul laughed and said, "I know. But this is a real paradise."

When they arrived at the island, Obaidul smiled triumphantly. "Didn't I tell you? Do you think God can make a better paradise than this?"

"I suppose not." Rurki was speechless for a little while. They were walking on the soft, white sand, hand in hand, sometimes lip to lip. Some trees were laden with flowers. Some were lush green, tall as if trying to reach the sky. There were lovely colourful birds everywhere. The forest and the sea made a very soothing sound. They were humming too while walking. Obaidul had not exaggerated a bit. The island was exactly like his description. They thought it would be a glorious seven days. Busy Obaidul could not spend more time than that. But he promised Rurki that they would come back again soon. They spent time loving each other. Practising every intricate position of the *Kama Sutra* and more. The Love and Lagoon restaurant had every sort of delicious food and drink. It was full of Eastern and Western promises and goodness. Eating there was a real treat for a few holiday-makers. The food, the atmosphere, the loveliness, the beauty – everything was too good to be true. Rurki had to think about her waist line.

Then she said, "But, with the number of calories we are burning each day, this shouldn't be a problem."

Odud replied, "No, my dear, it should not be a problem." He laughed heartily. "Like Marlon Brando, my American partner, Fredrick, bought a part of it. It's his Tahiti. Don't you think so?"

"I have not seen Tahiti, but your friend Fredrick must have good taste to invest in a place like this."

Obaidul told her the next day's plan. "I will swim for a long time here. Can you swim?"

"A little bit. But swimming in the sea is not for me. I would be scared to venture into the sea."

"When we go back, I will book you some swimming lessons. You can have a personal trainer and practice in our pool. Would you like that?"

"I would love that."

"Then the next time we two will swim together. You can even race me. Now let's go and eat. And after that I will have you as my sumptuous feast. Then you can sleep till eleven tomorrow. You'll be needing that when I finish with you." He gave a husky, rough smile. When Obaidul was at his hungriest, he smiled like that. "Join me when you feel nice and fresh tomorrow."

Rurki asked one awkward question. Perhaps it was a mistake, perhaps she was in a playful mood. "I am really surprised, Obaidul. With your huge sex appetite, why did you wait so long to get married again? Was it your guilty conscience?"

Obaidul's feet froze. That awkward question again! With chilling coldness, he answered, "When milk is cheap, why keep a cow?" Then he said in a serious, grave voice, "No guilty conscience. But,

Rurki, do not ask this sort of question again. I hope this is the last time. I warn you . . . ."

Rurki had not given much thought when she asked that question. But what could she do now other than utter "Sorry" a million times.

"Sorry, sorry, sorry!" She hugged him with a million kisses. Rurki begged, "Please do not be angry with me. Please do not spoil our fun."

The frozen legs got some life in them and he started to walk. He tried to explain why he hadn't married so long. "I was overjoyed to have met you, otherwise I can imagine being on my own for many years to come."

"I am sorry. So stupid of me to ask you an idiotic question." Her hands caressed every part of his body as she hugged him.

"Apology accepted." Hand in hand, lip to lip, they entered their chalet. In a stern voice, he uttered, "I hate those who call themselves intellectuals and pretend they know everything."

"Oh! Why have you brought up that subject now? Do you think I like them? Those long-haired Marxist vagabonds with baggy trousers and floral tops, with only some sugar-coated poems in their pockets? But no money? I hate them."

"Good!"

The one window which they had closed before going out was wide open. A cool Siberian breeze played a little, the pages of a book on the table rustled, the curtains billowed like sails. The breeze had disarranged the bedcover slightly and a lovely baby pink satin bedsheet was showing, telling them to make love, at once. After a minute or so, the Siberian breeze went out like a cloud of smoke through the window. Though Siberia was far away from this place, they could only compare the chill breeze with arctic weather.

Where did it come from? This terribly cool breeze? Rurki was surprised and perplexed. Obaidul was indifferent. He had other things on his mind, like which of the positions from *Kama Sutra* to practise. While they were travelling on an unbeaten track, that funny Siberian breeze entered through the overhead ventilator. Then swishing between them, it vanished again.

Next morning Obaidul had to leave the chalet early. He was a keen swimmer. He took a long, arduous swim. Then, feeling tired, he lay down on a beach towel and fell fast asleep. A cool breeze flew over his bare body for a little and as usual disappeared. Half awake, he murmured, "Fredrick never told me about this weather, about this funny cool breeze that comes and goes." Then he was fast asleep again.

With a basketful of fruits, sandwiches, cakes and drinks, Rurki came slowly to meet her husband. Her

Colossus of Rhodes was sleeping peacefully. Some spiderlike insects were playing on his open, broad face. But he did not know. He was sleeping so soundly. With her silk scarf, Rurki brushed the insects off his face.

Obaidul woke up and asked, "What is the matter, Rurki?"

"Nothing. Looked like some spiderlike insects were crawling on your face."

"Spiders!" he screamed. He had spider phobia. Severe arachnophobia which Rurki did not know anything about.

"Not exactly spiders. They just looked like spiders, that's all."

He sat up straight and started scratching his face like mad. With his nails he tried to peel the skin off his face. Then he stood up and continued to do the same.

Rurki hugged him, trying to calm him. She whispered softly, "You are such a baby. Please sit down and have some ice-cool drink. You will feel better for it." Then Rurki kissed him softly to soothe his nerves. But it took a while for him to get back to his normal self and sit down.

She asked, "How are you feeling now?"

Obaidul was reluctant to reply. Probably he was not sure how he was feeling.

Next morning Obaidul got up early. As he started to shave, he noticed some spots on his face. "God! What are they?"

"They are nothing but spots."

But Obaidul was not at all happy at Rurki's explanation. He became very restless.

"They are teenager's spots, silly. Don't you know that at heart you are still a teenager?"

"Teenager, my foot! I'm not staying here for a single night. We must leave this blasted paradise today."

Obaidul ignored his wife's lovely smile and her sense of humour.

As soon as they got back, they heard some bad news – his insane wife had commited suicide the day they left on their honeymoon. Her naked body was hanging from a ceiling fan. The shari she was wearing was her only way to freedom. Obaidul had to swallow two strong sleeping pills to get some sleep. He needed it badly.

Next morning at about 11 o'clock, Obaidul got up from bed. His head seemed heavy, and he was having difficulty seeing. He went to the big attached bathroom to put some cold water on his head and face. The big mirror was squeaky clean. He tried to gaze at his reflection in the mirror. He noticed those spots became big as summer boils on his face. His eyes were half-closed. With half-closed eyes, he stared at the mirror. He could hear a peculiar buzzing and wheezing sound inside those boils. As if something was trying its best to come out. He stared at his reflection in terror. And then pop! Out came baby spiders, thousands of them. They crawled on his face, under his vest, in his hair – everywhere.

Rurki came running to the bathroom door. The screams were sharp and loud like grenades blasting. Obaidul was screaming, screaming, screaming. Screaming his head off and dancing like mad.

"Obaidul, Obaidul, they are nothing. Just some baby spiders! Nothing! Listen to me, calm down."

But who was going to calm down and listen to his beloved wife? He was screaming just as his wife had ten years ago – screaming her head off.

His first wife was scared of snakes – a severe case of ophidiophobia.

He was scared of spiders – a severe case of arachnophobia.

Baby spiders were playing on his face and body happily as if they had found an ideal grazing field or playground. He went completely insane.

The cool Siberian breeze danced through the room and then went out through the window, probably to mix with the hanging clouds.

Rurki could not tell the good news of her pregnancy to her husband which she had realised only that morning. She herself had found it hard to believe. Petrified, Rurki looked for the nearest phone to call their physician. She mumbled, "Am I carrying his baby or spiders?"

Translated by Saleha Chowdhury

A Punk and Gulshan Ara

Gulshan Ara's office is closed today. The post office of this area remains closed on Thursdays. So, today is her holiday. As her children stay at school at this time, she finishes her shopping. She has been working as the counter clerk of the post office for ten years now. Her husband, Abdul Karim, does most of the weekly shopping, but there are a few things that he never buys. Gulshan Ara does not quite understand whether he forgets to buy them or he does so intentionally. Perhaps it's done deliberately. But she never quarrels with him for that and buys the stuff on her own. Abdul Karim pretends not to see anything as he does not want to ruin their peace by arguing about it. It is clear that the couple is peace-loving. Mr. Karim is reserved and Gulshan Ara is also not very talkative. She has stopped asking because she has not got any specific answer even after asking him several times. The things that Abdul Karim does not buy are beautiful tissue boxes, a fabric softener named Mist, a box of paper, a jar of branded coffee, Coffeemate, lace tablecloths, lace curtains, air fresheners, bathroom fresheners, etc. Her husband had once said, It's better if you buy the luxury stuff. She realises that all these are luxury items to her husband. She has to do the shopping of such small things for her children as well. She also buys both Abdul Karim's and her own favourite luxury items. He does not complain or snatch away her salary for this. She can probably be pointed out as one of the luckiest women in the world. Abdul Karim is quite solvent, he has a good salary. They do not get any holiday except when they visit their own country, and they do not have any luxury other than filling out the savings book. They do have satellite channels and video though. Both Gulshan Ara and Abdul Karim feel happy when they look at the savings book. Sometimes Gulshan Ara sends money to her aunts to buy food, milk and fruits. Abdul Karim does not have such matters to take care of. Their children study in a government school and they help them in their studies whenever they have some free time.

The last Thursday of May is bright and sunny. Summer is here! The luscious, green leaves of trees have made the park beautiful. The garden in her backyard is glowing with roses and tomatoes. Gulshan Ara becomes a bit extravagant in this weather. She has bought a shari for herself, a short-sleeved, printed shirt for Abdul Karim, T-shirts with pictures for the children, lace curtains for the kitchen and a lot of other stuff. Her hands grow tired carrying these things. She wants to give them some rest by sitting on the bench beside the street. She is as delighted as a child to have bought a *Cornetto* icecream. Good weather makes everyone happy without any reason. She observes the people walking past her. She remembers one or two other things while sitting on the bench. Although her hands are still aching, she stands up and decides to go to the shop after two bus stops. She catches the bus and takes out the shopping list once again. Looking out the window, she realises that the sky has become dark. Typical! The weather changes in the snap of one's fingers! Someone has said one should not trust the three W's: women, war and weather. Even if one does not agree with everything those male chauvinist pigs say, in Britain no one can avoid the last W. Actually, she is looking for a bright net curtain for the big, bay window of their living room. Some guests will come over to their place this Sunday. Moreover, the colours of the season have begun to play with her mind as well. So what if my load is heavy? she says to herself. I must take the curtains home today. She should have bought them after returning from her visit to Bangladesh.

As soon as she finishes her shopping, big raindrops start to fall. After a while, it starts raining heavily. She buys the biggest KitKat in the shop and enters a tea bar. Small tables and chairs are arranged in rows on both sides of the restaurant. There is a small aisle in the middle, with seats on both sides, like in an airplane. She wants to sit for a while as it is impossible to sit outside now. Perhaps it will not rain for long – just drizzle for some time. She looks everywhere. The whole tea bar is full – maybe because of the rain. Only one chair is empty at the table at the end. But a modern punk is sitting there with his spiked red hair, pierced nose and eyebrows, dangling safety pins in his ears. Aren't they called punks? She wonders what to do. She has no choice but to sit in front of the punk with pierced eyebrows and snake tattoos. She has to sit there even after seeing the hideous spikes. She hesitates for a while. But her hands and legs must have some rest. It takes a lot of courage to sit in front of a punk with pierced eyebrows and tattoos, even after living in this country for so long.

She gathers courage and takes her seat. The punk remains indifferent. She sets her things down by the chair and looks straight ahead. The punk or junk seems to be in a contemplative mood. She feels very hungry after the long walk from shop to shop and plans to eat the KitKat she has just bought. It's better not to eat anything from this restaurant. She does not like to stand in a long line to have tea or coffee. She looks at the line and divides the KitKat on the table into four. She notices that the punk or junk has stretched his hand to take half of the KitKat. He puts it in his mouth, very slowly. She looks at the spiky-red-haired guy in surprise. When she divides the second portion nicely into two more pieces, the young guy takes half of it and puts it into his mouth again. The punk does not take all of it, just half. The KitKat finishes. Both of them get equal portions. Do modern punks act like this? Eating what belongs to others? Although she feels annoyed, she does not want to say anything to the young man. She does not want to mess with him.

The sky is clearing. She does not have to sit here for long. She sees a small plate on the table in front of the punk. A big, white sugar-coated doughnut is lying on the plate. The guy has not touched the doughnut yet. She says to herself, "Eating others' food and then your own? Just see what I do to you!" She puts her three shopping bags together. Then she readjusts her shari a bit. She wipes off the KitKat crumbs from her lips. She puts on her shoes which were under the table. She stands up to go out. But, just a moment earlier, she had promised, "Just see what I do to you!" That's why, before the punk realises anything, she bites half of the doughnut and rushes out of the shop, leaving the rest of the doughnut on the plate. She rushes to catch the bus, afraid that the punk will follow her to the bus stop. Thank God! The bus swishes into the stop in front of her and she quickly jumps into it. Good job! She pats herself for being so bold. So? Will you eat other people's stuff again? But no one is following her. The shadow of the spiky-haired punk, with safety pins dangling from his ears, with pierced eyebrows and snake tattoos, is not behind her. Whew! She might have almost missed the bus, she laughs to herself.

The bus starts moving. She looks for her purse in the big cane basket. The purse seems to be way below, at the very bottom. She gets a shock as she reaches for her purse to pay for her ticket!

Her big KitKat is lying there quietly, deep down inside the basket.

Translated by Sabreena Ahmed

A Stopwatch and 400 Calories

"A correspondence secretary required for a former actress. Attractive remuneration with top-class board and lodging and other facilities will be provided. Candidates requested to apply with one recent photo and CV. P.O. Box 400, South Alabama."

As soon as he saw the ad, Subir Chowdhury decided to apply. Subir was intelligent. Back home, he had been quite well-known in the cricketing world. He had come to the States in search of his fortune. The ad seemed to be quite good. It did not seem that they would check his passport and green card. If he managed to get the job, he could enrol in night classes at some university and finish his studies.

He was staying with the family of a friend of his elder brother. He showed them the ad. The gentleman was doing quite well. He had two children. His wife did not do any job, but stayed at home. If anyone asked, "What do you do?" she would promptly reply, "Nothing. I don't do anything." As if looking after a family and bringing up two kids is nothing.

"Boudi," said Subir, "this ad looks interesting, doesn't it?"

Chitralekha read the ad. "A secretary to write letters? You might have to push around her wheelchair. The last years of celebrities are miserable."

"It may be something of that sort – responding to fan letters and pushing her wheelchair."

After putting her younger child to sleep, Boudi said, "You understand, board and lodging are free. There are also other perks. Go ahead, apply. Afterwards, when you're better off, you can always change jobs."

"You think so?"

"Of course. It doesn't matter whether or not you get the job. At least you'll have met a famous actress. And remember, Subir, the more interviews you face, the more knowledge you'll acquire. You'll get the experiences you need to stay here. At least it'll be better than the shoe store where you work now."

"If I get the job, " said Subir.

"Do one thing. Go to a studio and have a picture taken. Then prepare a good CV and send it off. Don't forget to write your extra-curricular activities – swimming, cricket, football. But don't write reading and singing."

"Why not?"

"Don't you understand? What will a former actress do with a secretary who likes to sing? All she needs is a strong man to push her chair about," Boudi said with a mysterious smile on her lips.

"Her chair?"

"It's the same – her wheelchair."

Subir decided to go to a photo studio, as Chitralekha Boudi suggested, and take a picture in the young Robert Redford style. "Date of birth" posed a problem. He was only twenty-three and a half. There was no way he could increase his age. If they wanted to see his birth certificate, they would know his age. Perhaps a former actress would not like someone so young. But Subir liked what Chitralekha Boudi had said, "The more interviews you face, the more knowledge you'll acquire." His elder brother's friend had to appear in at least a thousand interviews before he got a good job. He wanted to write a book about the interviews so that others would learn about the strange questions interviewers sometimes asked. Once an interviewer had asked him, "If you were left alone in a room full of snakes, what would you do?"

The candidate who said that he would hang on to the ceiling fan did not get the job. But the person who asked if the snakes were venomous got the job. The job had nothing to do with snakes or frogs at all. Nevertheless, such questions were being asked. Someone else had asked, "Which creature has not changed at all?" The person who answered "Human beings" did not get the job, while the person who answered "The crocodile" did. The crocodile has an auto immune system that cures its wounds. That's why it looks exactly the same as it did at the time of the Big Bang. The whole world of biology would turn upside down if scientists could learn the secret of the crocodile. These kinds of research papers help increase the knowledge of common people. This is what Indians do. Feed themselves and increase the knowledge of others.

It is like the question in a Satyajit movie, "What is the weight of the moon?" What does the weight of the moon have to do with what a clerk in the commercial bank ? But interviewers have the power to ask whatever they like. A thousand interviews and their twenty thousand questions would create a fantastic book. That is why Abhijeet Da had decided to write the book. Ironically, he had remembered all the answers the moment the interview was over. Hence, such a book would be invaluable to immigrants or ETs. Of course, he had not yet started writing, but every evening he shared his experiences with Subir.

A month after Subir applied for the job, he finally received a letter: "Congratulations! You are among our ten short-listed applicants. You are to come on the 13th of next month. Someone from our office will fetch you."

Subir was overjoyed. He might not get the job but the letter was typed on a letterhead with a golden monogram. It was obviously from someone very rich and famous. The letterhead was worth seeing: there were no words, just a golden design of leaves. He would get money, enjoy living in a palatial accommodation, experience the luxuries of Hollywood if somehow he got the job. And even if he did not get the job, he would at least have visited the mansion of a famous former actress for the interview.

The letter included some instructions: "Our car will pick you up from your house on the 13th at 8:30 am and bring you to the interview. We have to take these measures as outsiders are not allowed to enter this area, and the whole matter is highly confidential. Be ready and wait in front of your house. Don't forget to bring your identification papers with you."

Chitralekha Boudi cooked polao and duck with pineapple in honour of Subir. She had learnt the recipe from a Chinese resturant. Abhijeet Da recounted some more of his interview experiences. Subir wondered how a man could remember so much. Abhijeet was a good narrator. One could hear his stories again and again. Subir thought if the book ever came out, it would sell like hot cakes!

Subir dressed smartly for the interview. He had his hair cut at a good hair-dressing salon. He had a facial treatment afterwards as suggested by Chitralekha Boudi. He was ready to go then he stood in front of Boudi.

Boudi smiled. "You don't have to go anywhere. You can stay here as my helper in the kitchen – as Kitchen Assistant."

"I will always be that, Boudi, no matter what."

"You'll be free once you get the job. Alas! You won't step into this poor kitchen then. We won't even get to see your face."

"Let me get the job first, and then I'll keep aside some time to peep in here every now and again, Boudi."

In the microbus Subir got to see the other nine candidates for the job. It was a very nice four-wheeled microbus. Maybe the former actress used it whenever she needed to take a large group of people for an outing. The others in the car were silent.

With a pleasant smile Subir said, "Hello." It did not really matter if he failed the interview. He did not want to fight these nine gladiators to get the job. There was no doubt in his mind that he had everything a man needed to stay in the States. It looked as if the other nine men would starve if they did not get this glamorous job. They seemed to be thinking that no other offer in the world could be as generous and attractive as this one.

After driving through different roads, the car moved along a narrow path between two hills. The tall trees and the wild flowers nodded their heads merrily in the light breeze of April. The birds chirped in the branches while the butterflies flitted from flower to flower. After a little while, a white house came into view. It seemed to be standing alone on an open sea. Everyone shifted a little in his seat to get a glimpse of the house. All the men were handsome and smart, their ages between 25 to 30. Subir seemed to be the youngest of the group. Everyone had the same question in his eyes, "Is this the house?"

Subir asked the driver who had been driving silently all the way, "Are we heading towards this house? Will our interview be taken in this house?"

The driver answered without looking at Subir, "Yes."

"Is this our future employer's house?"

"One of her many houses." Saying this, the driver closed his mouth as if he would never speak again in his life.

The house seemed to dance in front of their eyes. It looked like a big swan guarded by countless green trees. Subir could not think of any other comparison at the moment. Some of the trees were covered with blossoms, others with shining green leaves.

One of the candidates asked, "Is this car also one of her hundred cars?"

"Sort of." The driver shut his mouth again.

They looked at the large house as the car slowly moved up the ascending road. They still did not know the name of the former actress. Was she Elizabeth Taylor or Brigitte Bardot? But they had heard that Brigitte Bardot lived in Paris with her ducks, hens, dogs, cats, cows, goats – and her latest husband. And beautiful Marilyn Monroe had breathed her last years ago. They could not think of the name of any other former actress. She could surely not be Demi Moore, Nicole Kidman, or Meryl Streep. Sophia Loren lived in her own villa in Italy. Sometimes the public got to see her picture on the front page of newspapers. And who did not know where Joan Collins was living with her toy-boy husband? "It might be Joan Collins," they thought. But the next moment they asked themselves, "How can that be?"

Who can this actress be? they kept on wondering. They were pretty sure that the driver would not say anything if he were asked.

The car stopped in front of the beautiful house. The house, which seemed milky-white from afar, had in fact a bluish tinge which highlighted the whiteness of the house even more. The whole house looked like a huge face – like John Steinbeck's house in Salinas Valley. It no longer looked like a swan. Suddenly, it seemed to have been transformed into an ancient human face – with two eyes and a nose – a face that had been gazing at the world since the beginning of time. Innumerable flowers bloomed in the garden. Which heaven did celebrities go to after they died? Could heaven be any better than this place? Perhaps the whole matter of life after death was metaphysical. It did not really matter where people went after they died but how they were.

The car proceeded up the path between the flowers and stopped under the porch. There was no one else to be seen. Then someone opened the door of the microbus and led them to a large room.

The sky-blue wall was nothing special. On one side there was a Lautrec; on the other hung a beautiful Matisse drawn in the Japanese style. A man was sitting at a big table in the room. He checked the identification papers of the candidates, who were then called one by one into the next room.

After everyone had been called to the next room, they were taken to a big swimming pool. One of the candidates was disqualified at this point, but the remaining nine swam in the pool. Subir was a very good swimmer. There were only a few good swimmers like him back in his country. But who could change his fortune swimming or playing cricket in that country? Subir dived into the swimming pool. He was badly in need of a job – he would welcome even the job of a clerk.

A number of surveillance cameras around the pool were directed at the swimmers. The actress had not come to meet them in person yet, but it was clear that she was observing all of them with the help of the cameras. After emerging from the swimming pool, they were taken to another room where they had to take a treadmill test. A man kept notes on how long each one of them lasted on the machines. Our twenty-three-and-a-half-year-old Subir beat them in this test as well. The others also did quite well; they were all very young – with hormones bubbling inside. Subir's youth was a plus point for him. He was more graceful and charming than the rest. The others had better physiques than Subir, with nugget-like muscles all over. Each one was a body builder and huge like a Roman gradiator.

Graceful and charming, Subir observed the other men. The appointed candidate would have to reply to fan letters. He could not understand why this mysterious and whimsical actress wanted them to swim and take a treadmill test! Maybe everyday he would have to push the former actress' wheelchair around the winding paths, up and down the mountains and valleys, and round the lake. Anyone doing such work had to be strong. Chitralekha Boudi guessed it right!

After a little rest, they were called one by one for the interview and paperwork. Subir knew all of the ten thousand interview experiences of Abhijeet Da. He did quite well in the interview. He had to check emails and write replies on the computer and show that he knew MS Word. Subir noticed the surveillance camera here also.

They were then invited to a sumptuous lunch. None of them had ever had such a lunch before. The men who did not get the job would at least remember this grand feast all their lives. They would never forget the items served along with caviar!

After this, they were called one by one. Subir did not know what the others were told. He was told that the actress would meet him in exactly seven days.

"Will the others come? I mean, the other nine candidates?"

"Five of them."

"On the same day?"

"No, on different days. She will take the interview herself on that day."

Subir asked, "Can I know her name?"

"No. She'll introduce herself."

They boarded the microbus again. The vehicle drove between the hills, leaving the house behind. It looked like a face, then it looked like a bird with its wings tucked in. After a while, the house was not visible anymore.

As soon as Subir reached home, Chitralekha Boudi asked, "Are you done?"

"I have to face another interview with Madam Butterfly herself."

"Oh! Is that her name? Madam Butterfly?"

"I don't know her name. It might be something like that, I guess. She'll introduce herself."

"I think you'll get the job. Do you want to give notice to the shoe shop now?"

"Not now. I just have to fit shoes on the feet of customers. Only a day's notice will do. Let me get the new job first. I'm fed up taking care of white, black, and brown feet all day long. Give me a break for God's sake!"

Boudi smiled. "A shoe shop is better than cleaning sewers. Your Abhijeet Da used to work in a sewerage company where he had to clean filthy drains and stinking sewers. But it's good that he didn't have to use his hands as the scavengers of our country have to. Here they use a machine to clean drains. Still, it's the same. I told my parents that their son-in-law worked as a sanitary inspector. Otherwise, wouldn't they have had a heart attack? Once he got a job where he had to sweep a supermarket. I told everyone at home that he was an industrial engineer." Chitralekha Boudi laughed.

Subir also joined in.

Boudi said, "He is truly an engineer now. But after a lot of odd jobs, my dear Subir." Boudi arranged her shari and continued, "If people ask, 'What do you do?' you can tell them that you're a sales executive. Why should you say that you are a shop assistant?"

"That's what I always say," Subir replied smilingly.

Seven days passed swiftly. "Does everyone buy more shoes in the spring?" wondered Subir. He did not get even a break for a sandwich. His ankles hurt because he had to crouch almost all day long; his back ached as well.

Subir took the day before the interview off so that he did not look like a tired immigrant, devastated by the everyday's war of life.

The car stopped in front of the swanlike, facelike, beautiful house. No one was there in the living room of the bluish-white house. The room had different pictures of the actress when she was young. Would she have looked so beautiful if the pictures had not been of her when she was young? He did not know about face lifts, bust lifts, botox, and the latest technique of cell replacement therapy. Or tummy tucks, nose jobs, chin implants, and other surgical procedures to maintain one's beauty. He did not even know about mud baths, milk baths, therapies, cell implants, and hundreds of such strange stuff at that time.

The whole atmosphere of the room changed when she entered. He could not recall if he had seen her before in any movie. She had a curvaceous body. He guessed she was about five feet five inches and weighed eight stone as she sat down on the chair in front of him. Her eyes were a rare blue and her teeth were like beautiful white pearls. She was wearing a sea-green dress and slippers. Her breasts were firm and attractive.

"I'm Vivien Leigh," the actress introduced herself.

Subir was astonished at hearing the name. Vivien Leigh was dead! And even if she were alive, she would be about 80.

"I faked my death," said the actress. "I did this to escape fans."

"Are you the Vivien Leigh who played the role of Scarlett O'Hara in *Gone with the Wind?*"

"Why does everyone keep asking the same old question?"

"But you look like...."

"That's the gift of modern science and stem cell replacement therapy. There are many other things that you needn't know, Subir."

Two crystal glasses and a beautiful bottle of champagne appeared in between their tête-à-tête, as if from a hanging garden somewhere.

"Let's celebrate. Cheers," said Vivien Leigh.

"What are we celebrating?"

"Your job. Your future with me. You've come such a long way – all these things. But before that . . . . Okay, forget about it. Drink!"

As Subir sipped the champagne, a soft wave seemed to ripple all over his body. He did not know what had been put in the drink, but it aroused him. As it did Vivien Leigh! They talked and laughed and were soon sitting on the same sofa. Vivien Leigh's perfume had diffused all over the room. Her golden hair covered Subir's body. Each lock of hair seemed to have spread its hood like the snakes of Medusa to entangle his whole existence. All his inhibitions melted away. Vivien Leigh whispered so seductively that Subir's control over his senses dissolved into the air like an untamed horse. He was ready to gallop now. Vivien Leigh had been waiting for exactly this moment. Her pert nose brushed against his earlobes as her wicked tongue tasted him bit by bit – first his neck, then his shoulders and back. She showered Subir with her small kisses, as if sipping his body. Subir's burning desire melted Vivien Leigh down with its horse power. She took out a stopwatch and placed it beside them. Subir did not notice the stopwatch as he had already lost himself in the labyrinth of Medusa's snakes.

He drowned into her, then floated up again, and drowned again.

He kept on floating and drowning endlessly.

Engaged in that mad and wild passion, Subir lost track of time.

After the game was over, they lay naked on the sofa. Vivien Leigh picked up the stopwatch and held it up. She gave a satisfied smile and said, "I was right about you. Fifty-five minutes. Five more minutes to complete one full hour. That's manageable."

Her eyes seemed to sparkle more than before. Maybe she had had a fresh injection of botox to rejuvenate her rose-petal skin. She looked so innocent.

"An hour's sexual activity burns a total of 400 calories. Three times this activity during the day and night help to burn 1,200 calories. Burning calories by exercising is so boring and out-dated! And I love to eat, you know! If I consume 1,200 calories after this, then I'm left with only 1,200 calories which is the minimum an adult needs. An elderly person may have other dietary restrictions, but I am happy with this calculation. 1,200 more for the 1,200 used up calories. That's a hell of a lot of calories! I think I can even eat a tub of vanilla icecream everyday. Exercise? No, I can't even bear to think about it. In the near future, I believe this exercise business will disappear. Many people are fed up of swimming, running on tread mills, cycling, aerobics. But this is fun!" Vivien Leigh used her legs as forceps to grab Subir in such a manner that he felt like helping her lose 400 more calories right at that moment! But he threw her off and sat up. He stared at her face. He had heard that Vivien Leigh's husband, Sir Laurence Olivier, had to drag men from the street to quench her insatiable hunger. And now she wanted to pay a man to maintain her everyday workouts.

"Sometimes husbands get a huge compensation for divorce. When my seventh husband fell in love with my maid and wanted a divorce, I had to give him a million pounds and a house. He had threatened to disclose all my secrets. But I'm planning to call a press conference after twenty years or so to tell everyone about my life. I'll be an example of 'A living success of the magic of plastic surgeons and cell therapy.' Everyone should know that youth need not end. It can be eternal."

Subir asked, "Does that mean that I have to be your secretary for the next twenty years?"

"How old are you?"

"Twenty-three years and six months."

"No, I don't sleep with anyone who's over thirty-five, specially those who have grey hair on their chests. You'll stay with me for five or seven years. After that, fresh meat."

Vivien Leigh gave a mischievous smile. She reached out her hand for another glass of champagne. Who knew what was mixed with the champagne that came floating in? All his values and senses had evaporated into air because of that champagne.

Subir asked, "Have you interviewed anyone else?"

"I interviewed only one other person. He was okay, a real gladiator. He took an hour and five minutes in the first round. And fifty minutes in the second round. He is the second best. You're meat of a different flavour. Though Indians wrote the *Kama Sutra*, they are not famous in this field. But you're wonderful, flawless like the creation of a sculptor! I love arts and aesthetics."

Subir stood up and said, "Can I leave now? When do I join?"

"Whenever you wish."

"After seven days, then."

"That's fine." Vivien sipped her champagne. "Soon, we won't need the stopwatch anymore. You'll be an expert."

"With your blessings!"

"You have my blessings."

Subir changed his residence. Who knew when Vivien Leigh's driver might not pop up to kidnap him? Indians were not famous. But Vivien Leigh ignored the many Indians who had won the Nobel Prize. Though the salary and perks of the job were pretty good, the proud Indian Subir did not want to work as a gigolo or male prostitute.

"Hello, Subir, have you been able to get a good job?" Subir's father asked, his voice muffled over the card phone.

Subir answered, "Baba, I'm still a sales executive."

Subir Chowdhury was a bloody damn liar!

Translated by Sabreena Ahme

Desdemona's Handkerchief

Mohor starts her day with a cool morning shower. It refreshes her body. She stands in the room with her hair wrapped in a towel. Her face is wet. The water dripping from her eyelashes seems like dewdrops sliding down leaves. She wipes her face with her *anchal*. Abul Hossain has finished reading the newspaper and is now solving a crossword puzzle. Usually he has toast and fruit for breakfast. Then he relishes his first cup of tea, sweetened with condensed milk. He holds the cup and looks down at his feet. Laily has curled up snugly and fallen asleep there. A red bell dangles from the red floral ribbon round Laily's neck. She also has a plate, red like the ribbon. A little piece of toast and tea have been her breakfast too. She always has a portion of whatever Abul Hossain eats throughout the day. Crumbs of his breakfast, lunch and dinner are showered on her plate. She even gets to eat a 5 o'clock snack with him. Earlier, Radha used to have these privileges like Laily. And Urvashi had enjoyed her stay here before Radha came.

Abul Hossain caresses Laily tenderly and announces, "After Laily's death, I want to name the new one Juliet."

A light purr of gratitude comes out of Laily's throat in response. Abul Hossain then mutters to himself, "And it has to be a female. I love female cats."

Laily's purrs show that she is listening to him. Mohor has also heard his words − as usual in her unresponsive way. Her expressionless face never shows any sign of listening to anything attentively. She always seems to be in a trance or a dream world. "Are you done with your bath?" Abul Hossain looks at Mohor and asks.

As she pulls the towel from her head, her dark hair cascades down her back. Her hair is so beautiful even at this age! She has thick, curling eyelashes, dark tresses of hair, and a pair of amazing eyebrows. She is the cloud-queen on a rainy day.

"I'm done," she replies.

A few grey tresses peep out of her hair to remind her of the number of bygone seasons of her life. So many winters, summers, springs and rains have passed. For a moment she stares at the woman in the mirror holding a comb. Then she quickly combs her hair and rubs moisturiser on her face. She ends with a touch of *kajal* to her eyes and a tiny ladybird *teep* of *kumkum* between her eyebrows. Mohor loves to spruce herself a little in front of the mirror. The feeling of looking at your own face is amazing! She looks at herself in the mirror one last time before returning to Abul Hossain.

"What are we having for lunch today?" he asks, while trying to coax Laily to have another bit of toast.

"Don't feed her any more. She's already had enough. She'll die of a heart attack if you keep feeding her all this stuff. Radha died because of excess fat around her heart. Don't you remember? Someday Laily will also have the same fate."

The powder Mohor uses has a sandalwood fragrance. It announces her presence to Abul Hossain. He says, "What's wrong if she eats a bit of toast?" He does not lift his eyes from Laily.

Mohor screws up her eyes and observes the cat. "I'm saying it because I'd have to house-train a new one if she dies all of a sudden."

Mohor moves to the window of the living room. The birds on the branches of the *arjun* tree are merry on this sunny day of spring. A swift breeze brushes against her *teep* and slowly licks the sandalwood flavoured body all over.

She says, "What a wonderful day!"

Instead of responding to her ecstatic utterance, Abul Hossain asks, "What are we having for lunch?"

Beef is never brought into the house as Abul Hossain does not like it. They usually have fish and vegetables. Abul Hossain can only see Mohor's back now.

She continues to look out of the window while replying, "*Potol dolma* and *shorputi* fish."

"What happened to the green peas we had yesterday?" Abul Hossain loves green peas.

"All of it was put in the *khichuri*. But there is some cauliflower. I'll fry it with a chickpea batter. You relish that."

For the last twenty-six years, these two have lived under the same roof. Mohor goes to the garden to pluck fresh tomatoes and green chillies. As she goes outside, Abul Hossain moves towards Mohor's closet full of cosmetics.

Bottles.

Cans.

Containers.

Jars.

Anti-wrinkle moisturiser.

Mohor has mixed some oil with the moisturiser. It's not just any ordinary oil. She has pierced vitamin E capsules and stirred the oil into the cream. These precious lotions and potions will prevent wrinkles. No crow's feet or laughter lines will dim the beauty of her dark eyes. This special skin care has proved to be quite fruitful. The creases around her lips disappear as soon as she smiles. Abul Hossain looks at the newspaper over his glasses and remarks, "It's clever to stay young forever. Who knows what it can bring you?"

Even after twenty-six years of marriage, Mohor has to listen to all these sarcastic remarks. She does not respond to his taunts. Only the breeze that has been soothing her soul suddenly turns rough and whirls through the room. Her face does not show any sign of bitterness. Abul Hossain's high-powered glasses cannot see what she has deep in the core of her heart beating under her blouse. He cannot see it even when he tears off the hooks of Mohor's blouse while making love. Mohor is always delighted to see her own reflection in the mirror. She is so happy that she feels like presenting herself a lovely gift. May be a bottle of perfume.

To Abul Hossain, Mohor always seems to be in a trance. She does not even come to her senses while quarrelling with him. The remark made to her a few minutes earlier does not seem to bother her much. She wipes the border round the *kumkum teep* with her *anchal*. Then she looks at herself closely in the mirror and goes to her own room. The house has an extra room which Mohor uses as her study. She reads books and listens to songs in that room. Sometimes she rocks herself on the rocking chair and takes a flight to the world of imagination. Then she lies on the flooe on her back and keeps staring at the ceiling fan. She buys magazines for both men and women. Reading these magazines for a long time is another pastime of Mohor's. Abul Hossain is fifty-eight, Mohor just fifty-two. Abul Hossain has now retired and can keep an eye on his wife all day long. Mohor spends some time on her own in the next room where her husband's eyes cannot follow her. This special time is not long though.

After having her bath, she reads books. In a little while, her eyes droop with sleep. But Abul Hossain becomes restless and calls her from the next room in a loud voice. Mohor ties her hair into a loose bun and goes to him.

"Why can't you stay in front of my eyes? Are you disgusted that you have a husband with eczema?"

Abul Hossain's rivets her olive-smooth body with his gaze.

Mohor avoids answering his question and says, "Would you like some tea?"

Abul Hossain notices that her face has puffed up as if she has been sleeping. And he has been lying here with his rough skin.

He continues, "Am I responsible for this skin disease?"

"Shall I bring some of your favourite digestive biscuits with tea?"

"Only tea."

Abul Hossain snatches the cup from her hands.

A fat lizard is walking on the wall near the calendar of a *shari* shop. Its belly is stuffed with eggs. Mohor is not as lucky as the lizard − she could not be a mother.

Though Abul Hossain has refused to have anything with tea, he grabs the plate of digestive biscuits brought by Mohor. He dips the biscuits in the tea. Both Abul Hossain and Laily munch on the biscuits.

"You're giving her biscuits and tea again?"

"I can't eat anything without worshipping the cat. Why do you keep asking this? You know everything!"

Mohor does not say anything.

She sits on the sofa in front of him. The Falgun wind is ushering out winter. She takes the ball of knitting needles and wool from the table and starts knitting a sweater.

After finishing his tea, Abul Hossain picks up the ointment prescribed by the dermatologist. He tries to put it on his rough skin but cannot reach his back. He says, "Come here. I can't reach my back."

Mohor gets up and goes to sit beside him. While rubbing the ointment on his back, she says, "Your back has almost healed." Then she pulls his vest down and goes towards the bathroom to wash her hands.

"Where are you going?"

"To the bathroom. I have to wash my hands, don't I?"

Abul Hossain frowns at her. "You are scared that you'll get my disease also, isn't it?"

Mohor opens her sleepy eyes wide and says, "Just the two of us live here in this house. Would it be right to suffer from the same disease deliberately?"

Abul Hossain kicks at Laily's belly hard and says, "Get lost!'

After washing her hands well, Mohor enters the kitchen. She will now listen to songs and cook the *potol dolma* and *shorputi* fish and fry the cauliflower dipped in chickpea batter. She will rest after putting up the rice in the rice cooker. The song goes on and so does Mohor's humming.

Abul Hossain knows what kind of wife does not stop singing while her husband is rotting with a stinking skin disease and acidity. He also knows who uses beautifying moisturisers at this age. But Mohor the housewife does not go out that much.

Her sleepy eyes look down at the food she is cooking for lunch. What song is she singing? "*Je raatey mor duar guli bhanglo jhore. . . .*That stormy night when all my doors broke. . . . "

"Bullshit!"

After serving food on the table, Mohor calls her husband, "Come, lunch is served."

If Mohor takes a bath in the morning, she does not take another before lunch. Once in a while, she cools herself under the shower before going to bed at night. Laily is served on the red floral plate first. Then Abul Hossain reaches for his first morsel of rice. "I'll start after you, Laily."

He asks Mohor, "Do you see Shudhamoy these days?"

For a moment, Mohor's sleepy eyes burn fiercely. She answers with her head low, "No."

"Never?"

"Never." She answers him in monosyllables on this matter.

Twenty-five years ago, Abul Hossain was feeling out of sorts. He came home early and stopped at the entrance. He listened silently to the conversation going on inside. He usually did not return home at that time.

"Why have you come again, Shudhamoy?"

"To see you, Mohor."

Thousands of kisses caressed Mohor's lips, eyes, cheeks and body. Shudhamoy had clasped Mohor passionately in his arms. "Only to see you, Mohor, for no other reason."

"To see me? But . . . . "

The man named Sudhamoy did not let her finish her sentence and sealed her lips with his. After a while Mohor managed to free herself from his embrace and said, "There was no news of you after you went to Vietnam. Besides, you are Shudhamoy Sen and I am Mahjabeen Mohor. It was impossible for us to be together. Could we have broken the norms of society? Tell me! "

From the other side of the door, Abul Hossain could guess that Mohor was in Shudhamoy's arms again. He would not have come if he had not had this terrible headache. The conversation paralysed him.

"Don't come here anymore, Sudhamoy."

"Why not?"

The sound of kisses numbed Abul Hossain.

"Because I am married. . . ."

Abul Hossain moved away from the door and went out to have some fresh air. Then he returned to stand beside the slightly ajar door again. The couple were not speaking much now. It seemed that one was crying while the other was wiping away the tears.

Shudhamoy said, "How can I live without seeing you, Mohor?"

They opened the door of the room and were as shocked as if they were seeing a ghost at seeing Abul Hossain.

The next scene took place outside the house. The two men were on the street. Abul Hossain was mad with rage. He only said, "If you come here again, it won't be good for Mohor."

"I won't come again."

"Promise?"

"I promise."

After Shudhamoy left, Abul Hossain did not go back to the house directly. He went to a nearby pet shop named "The Golden Fish" and bought a cat. He brought it in a cage and announced indifferently, "From today I begin to worship my cat. All the stuff you cook for me, I will serve her first. I am naming her Urvashi."

Surprised, Mohor stood there in silence. Her sad eyes tried to understand the mystery of the cat. She had learnt about the ritual of worshipping the cat. She knew the reason behind such worship, but did not say anything. That night, Abul Hossain devoured Mohor's body with his bestial lust and said, "Bastard! Can that Shudhamoy of yours be like me in bed?"

Mohor rushed to the bathroom to wash away the marks of his paws and poisonous teeth from her body. She kept sitting in the dark to stay away from him. This was the beginning and the end of his devouring process. On entering the room again, she could see the burning light of Abul Hossain's cigarette in the dark.

He asked in a cold manner, "Why didn't your parents tell me about your affair with that *malaun(hindu)* before our marriage?"

Mohor lay down on the bed with her face towards the wall. She had to answer these questions against her will. "They did not know about it."

"Why didn't you tell them?"

"They didn't ask for my opinion."

What then? Twenty-six years of their marriage had survived the wear and tear of such quarrels and hate.

After finishing his meal, Abul Hossain observes Mohor closely. She is chewing the fish bones intently – even the mention of that Vietnamese bomb named Shudhamoy does not bother her much. Mohor is exactly like Laily. She forgets everything while chewing fish bones. She seems to be hypnotised. Abul Hossain bangs his glass loudly on the table. Still she does not come out of her own world. He cannot stand it any longer and drops the plate on the floor. Mohor stands up and cleans the shattered pieces of the plate from the floor. They got rid of the double bed last year. One day Abul Hossain was surprised to see the new twin beds side by side in their room. Mohor's father was a teacher who had saved a little money for his daughter. She had managed it with that money.

"What happened to the double bed?"

"Its leg was broken. I sold it and bought these. Moreover, now your body . . . . "

Abul Hossain feels like burning Mohor with the fire of his raging eyes. "My body? This is only a temporary thing! Do you think that all the doctors and *kabiraj* have vanished from the face of the earth?"

"We'll buy a big bed as soon as you get well."

"Whom do you wish to think of lying on the other bed?"

"Oh! A sleepyhead like me? The moment I lie down on the bed, I fall asleep." Mohor yawns while replying.

In the bluish-green light of the night, Abul Hossain can guess that Mohor is laughing to herself.

"You mock my body! Why? Didn't you get pleasure from it all these years?"

"Are you out of your mind?" As she says this, Mohor drowns in the sea of deep sleep. And her deep sighs make the air of the room heavy.

"What are you doing in the afternoon?" Mohor wants to know if he will go to his friend's place to play chess. Sometimes he goes there to pass the afternoon.

"You'll be free when I go out, isn't it? You can think of whoever you want when I'm not here."

"It's better to have a few friends. How can one spend the whole of one's retired life looking at the face of only one person?"

That's right. It does not feel good to look at only one person all the time. He notices that Mohor has painted her nails. Maybe she will go to the shop to buy some cosmetics when he goes out.

Abul Hossain does not want to admit that he cannot tolerate Mohor being out of his sight even for a moment. Sometimes Mohor feels suffocated by the bonds of marital life. Sometimes she is so tired that she falls asleep like Laily and cannot wake up. She does not know why it happens. Maybe, her subconscious mind does not want to live in this harsh reality.

When she opens the writing pad to write something, Abul Hossain peeps over her shoulders. "What are you writing?"

"Nothing special."

Still, Abul Hossain leans over the writing pad to see closely. Even a single breath of Mohor cannot escape Abul Hossain's ears. Can her writing be any different? When her breath turns into a sigh, Abul Hossain becomes angry.

She wants to draw a lake. All the birds which are afraid to come to her garden will sing in that garden. She might even draw a complicated knitting pattern or write a recipe.

"All this feminine stuff. Snivelling, crying and whining!"

Mohor does not react to his remarks. She keeps on doing what she has. But Abul Hossain suddenly has a terrible headache and Mohor has to put eau-de-cologne on his temples. When he closes his eyes to rest, she puts away the writing pad in the drawer and goes to the other room. As soon as she leaves the room, Abul Hossain opens his eyes and goes to the bathroom. Then he opens up all the jars, bottles and cans of cosmetics and anti-wrinkle moisturisers. He scrapes dead skin from his eczema-infected body and mixes it with the moisturisers.

"Ish! What a way to stay young forever!" Stretching your hands above your head and reaching for your feet in the morning. Moving the neck in a circular movement and swinging the waist from side to side.

Why does she want to stay young? Because the sun still rises to glorify mother earth. Because the birds still sing to soothe one. Because the blue sky is covered with grey clouds when rain is imminent. Isn't just living in this world is beautiful?

Abul Hossain does not know what Mohor's heart under her *anchal* desires the most. Maybe, Mohor herself does not know what she wants. Abul Hossain can feast on her body with his indomitable lust, but can he ever possess her heart with his love-making?

Sometimes Mohor bathes for the second time when his passion is satiated. Then she sits under the light of the floor lamp. Her red, painted toes shine under that light. Tears fill her eyes as someone else's face comes into her mind . . . She tries to reach out to him in the light . . . and slowly lowers her hands again . . . folding them on her bosom.

Abul Hossain crosses the room to go to the bathroom.

"Aren't you coming back to the room?"

"Coming."

Like the extra furniture of the house, the trees of Mohor's mind become stiff and frigid on most nights. She lies on the single bed of her study and feels relieved to think that Abul Hossain will not be able to own her now. It's a test of herbal medicine. She is happy to see the benefits of *salsa* prescribed by the *kobiraj*.

Suddenly, one day, Laily passes away like Radha. All these foods has made her fat and lazy. Too much of Abul Hossain's adoration has brought early ageing and inevitable death. A piece of toast is stuck in her mouth still. The poor thing could not even sip the tea poured into the saucer for her.

Urvashi had passed away, then Radha and now Laily. Abul Hossain orders Mohor angrily, "Bring me a cat from 'The Golden Fish' right now. They always keep a stock of cats."

Mohor cannot restrain her tears while burying Laily in the corner of the garden. Radha and Urvashi are also sleeping here under the shade of the guava tree. No attitude of Abul Hossain has ever surprised Mohor. But this time, she cannot understand how a man does not utter a word of grief at the death of his favourite pet. How can he let go of his best friend so calmly? Mohor looks at the cane basket where Laily used to sleep. Oh! The poor thing. She covers her eyes with her *anchal*. Abul Hossain does not even know that Mohor has the habit of crying amidst her laughter and laughing amidst her tears.

"When are you going to the pet shop?" Abul Hossain asks impatiently. "When are you bringing a cat for me?"

He has not been going out for the past few days because of a cold and flu. Mohor knows exactly what he will say now. He will say that he cannot eat anything without worshipping the cat.

"I'll change my clothes and then go to the market. I have to buy some stuff also."

"What stuff?"

"Some vegetables, eau-de-cologne for you and sandalwood powder for me."

She takes a shari from the almirah and drapes it around herself. It seems that she is going to a party rather than the market. The blue *jamdani* shari has a red polka dot design. The red *teep* glows on her forehead like a dot of sunlight. Her sandalwood fragrance disperses in the air like incense. The neatly tied bun on her head is also very beautiful. She grabs a purse and a plastic bag. She can manage quite well with the little amount of money in her hands. Complaints? Housewife Mohor has never complained about Abul Hossain's meagre income.

"Don't be late. I'm not feeling well. Come home quickly."

"I will."

Mohor disappears round the corner of the lane. She walks past men and women on both sides of the street, rows of green trees, honking cars and quite a few shops before reaching the entrance of the pet shop.

Someone grabs her and pulls her towards him, "Come here." The voice is calm.

The freelance journalist has not changed at all. Shudhamoy is standing in front of the pet shop called "The Golden Fish."

"So, Mr. Freelance Journalist, what brings you here?"

"What brings you here to the pet shop, Mohor?"

A sudden chill runs through Mohor's body.

"Shudhamoy? But why?"

"I'm Shudhamoy. Can you recognise me?"

He sniffs the fragrance of sandalwood near her neck and whispers, "Don't you know me?"

Shudhamoy can tell when Mohor is here by her special sandalwood smell. The same red *teep* on her tiny little forehead. Her *teep* had spread on his white *kurta* many times. He notices the age wrinkles around her eyes and lips. These were not there when he had last taken her into his arms.

He strokes each of the wrinkles with his fingers and asks, "Why have you come here again?"

Mohor does not say anything. She is standing close to Shudhamoy. She touches his cheeks and asks, "Don't you know why?"

"I know. You've come here to buy a cat."

"How did you know?"

"I know everything you do. I've given him twenty-five years. But I can give him no more."

"We have only a few years to live, Shudhamoy."

"Exactly, only a few more years."

"You've completed sixty and I've completed fifty," Mohor smiles sweetly.

"Yes, I have." Sudhamoy looks deep into her eyes.

"I'm happy, Shudhamoy, you don't know . . . ."

"Shshsh! You don't even know how to tell a lie. So don't try it!"

He moves her worn-out bangles up and down her arms. Mohor's eyelids tremble as she submits herself to his embrace.

"Listen, Mohor, go with me. We should not waste anymore of our time. You're right. We are here in this world for only a few years."

"Where?"

"If we walk fast, we can reach the station and catch the next train."

"Where will we go?"

"Wherever I go."

"But you roam around all over the world."

"You'll also roam with me." He holds her hand. "Let's go. Why are you thinking so much?"

"Who'll cook for him? He doesn't know how to cook."

"He'll cook himself. And before eating the meal, the cat . . . ."

Mohor covers his lips with her palm, "Don't say it."

Mohor's sleepy eyes sparkle with the lightning of life. Has a flicker of existence blazed in her after exactly twenty-five years?

"I haven't brought anything with me."

"Who told you that you need to bring anything?"

"Your God and my God. All these obstacles."

"There is a God in your soul and there is a God also in my soul. Beside them there's another God who rules the path of one's journey and its speed. Let's bow our heads in His honour."

Shudhamoy holds Mohor's hand tightly. A purse full of coins and a plastic bag remain lying on the ground in front of the pet shop.

"Walk a bit faster. We'll miss the train."

Mohor holds on to Shudhamoy's hand and tries to walk faster.

"You're limping, Shudhamoy. Have you hurt yourself?"

"Yes, a bit. The pain will go away now. I've been dreaming of holding your hands and reaching the platform . . . a sweet journey with my beautiful Mohor . . . a destination. And you see, we are living that dream now!"

Mohor trembles once again.

Abul Hossain looks out of the window. Mohor is walking briskly towards the house, holding the cage tightly in her hand. Flowers adorn her hair and wrists; on her lips she wears a sweet smile. She seems to be hypnotised. She wants to reach home quickly.

Abul Hossain cannot find any difference between Mohor and the lifeless furniture of his house. On the other hand, Mohor's world of imagination and reality merge. She cannot separate one from the other.

Translated by Sabreena Ahmed

A Sumptuous Lunch

Molly Fisher was one of over nine million pensioners in Great Britain. She lived in the same tiny council flat for the last thirty years. She had to pay some rent and a reduced council tax. She had not been working all her life. So she could not stick all the stamps one could on the government's ledger book for a big pension. As a result her pension was meagre. She tried her best to manage with the little money she got. She was not alone in Britain. Lots of pensioners were like her. If they had a small pension with a flat or a house to stay in old age, they considered themselves lucky. If they didn't have any, they ended up in a care home.

Molly was seventy-five when this story unfolded. She was fairly healthy. Occasionally, however, her swollen legs troubled her. The doctor told her, "It is a kind of gout, Molly. You better learn to live with it. I'm afraid there isn't any real cure for it but to ease the problem I can give you something. You watch your steps and be careful." She watched over her steps and always tried to hide her legs in trousers. She had to do some walking – shopping, going to the laundry, meeting friends, going to church and, for a bit of fun, window shopping. She was a happy-go-lucky sort of person. So no one saw her swollen legs and misery that much. She was good at covering up everything.

Twenty-five years ago her only son James emigrated to South Africa. He had a wife and two children, and he seemed to be doing well there. Molly used to get two cards a year from her only son – one on Christmas and one on her birthday. For the rest of the year, she never heard from James. Her husband had died thirty-five years ago of alcoholism. An Irish man, he did not earn much. He was just a fitter – fitting other people's taps and showers. A lazy type of person, whose only joy was drinking. After his death, Molly started to get some pension as his widow, it was more than the money her husband used to give her. Molly had to pay the electric bill, gas bill, water bill as well as rent and council tax. She had one insurance for her boiler and radiators. She did not have that insurance for a long time. But one day her boiler broke down. It was January – a very cold winter. The repair man who showed his card and pretended to be an engineer was a fraud. He was a con who tricked her to pay for the repairs and a new boiler. Poor Molly had to sell her only expensive possession – a pair of gold and ruby bangles to pay the bill. A third-class con robbed her one and only treasure. Her three friends, Ruth, Pauline and Vera, told her, "Insure your heating system, Molly. For future security you be needing that. We know you have to pay the money for the insurance monthly but it would be a lot better than what you faced this time." Molly listened to them and another extra bill was added with the others.

All those bills went up every year in Britain. But the pensions never went up at the same rate. After she learnt that pensions increased every year in April, she phoned her friend, Ruth. "Only two pounds a week better off now. How am I going to pay all the bills which have gone up like rockets? We cannot stretch out two pounds to two hundred, not even twenty. What does the government think of us? That we are magicians?"

"Yes. We are magicians. Don't you know that, Molly? Look out for a Royal Mail special delivery. The government is sending us a magic wand to do our job properly."

"You look out for that parcel containing a magic wand. I think I won't be eating from now on. If I do, only bread and water."

"Me too." Ruth, who giggled a lot, became serious.

So Molly had to think twice even about spending a penny. She had been a cleaner at a school. When anybody asked about her profession, she replied laughing, "I was an industrial engineer." Maybe for that reason her tiny flat looked squeaky clean. In Britain, National Health takes care of everybody's health. So free medical care saved her life and money. But she always wished, how wonderful it would be if I could visit a chiropodist privately. But her wish was only a wish; she could not afford to make that wish a reality. So Molly and her bad legs survived somehow.

Molly had two hobbies. Once a week she loved to go the town hall to play bingo with Ruth, Pauline and Vera. And once a month she loved to visit her hairdresser. Once she had masses and masses of hair. But now to cover the bald patches, she had to do some colouring, curling and waving. When the hairdresser finished her job, she looked at the mirror and smiled happily at her reflection.

Her birthday was the same as the Queen Mother's – 4th of August. After a lot of searching, she had found one similarity with the Queen Mother – both of them loved bread and butter pudding.

"The Queen Mother got a new hip when she was ninety. Will I get one at ninety?" she asked Vera.

"You get a wheelchair, darling, if you are lucky and live that long."

"No new hip for me?"

"You can rest your hips in a wheelchair in a care home." Vera never giggled. She was always serious. "I think I will have one too. Then we can have a wheelchair race."

"I'm looking forward to it."

Then both of them laughed a little.

Molly always laughed her heart out, talked her lungs out, and sang her vocal cords out. And when she cried, her cloud of emotions sometimes rained bucketful of salt water. Three incidents made her cry like that. She categorised those three as sensible and bloody stupid. Two were sensible but one was bloody stupid. The two sensibles were when she had to sell her gold and ruby bangles for the fake engineer, and when her only son James forgot to send her a birthday card. The third bloody stupid one was when she thought she saw Paolo. One day when she was seventy-two, she was standing at a bus stop. It was raining heavily. She noticed a man with a hooded raincoat walking fast. Good Lord! It's Paolo. Paolo had been her teenage sweetheart. She called as loudly as she could, "Paolo! Paolo!" Paolo's lookalike never turned back to answer her call. "How could Paolo ignore me? Once Paolo wanted to die for me." And then . . . . She did not wait for the bus. She returned home, went straight to bed, and cried a bucketful of salt water. "Have you forgotten me, Paolo? How could you?" Her emotion of clouds turned into torrential rain. The clouds cleared as she was healthy in body and mind. If I'm seventy-two, Paolo would be seventy-five by now. But that man with the hooded raincoat looked exactly the same as Paolo at twenty-one.

Later on she called it, "My silly stupid emotion."

I have to mention here that Englishwomen never cry like that. They are sort of the *Quo Vadis* type. They do not look for goblets to save their tear drops as Nero did in the film, but a small tissue is good enough for that purpose. But Molly was not all English. Her mother was Italian. So her emotional behaviour was a bit different.

But wasn't crying for a missing birthday card from her only son James silly? It was always only a card. Nothing inside the card. No rands or pounds. If James had done that she could have bought that floral dress which she admired so much while window shopping or some similar thing. She reasoned with herself that crying for a missing card was not silly. "He is my only son. I have got every right to cry." It seemed half-Italian Molly was not like a typical English woman.

On her birthday, she religiously invited her three friends to a nice pub and told them, "Have a glass of wine on me and crisps." She made the place bright with her hearty smile. In return she used to get some small presents, -like a bar of sweet-scented soap, a small jar of bubble bath, a bottle of sunblock cream to protect her skin from the bright sun when sunbathing at the local park. She wished to do something better for her birthday but never could afford it.

After Christmas she sometimes phoned her friends, "You get lovely presents from your daughters, Ruth. They never forget you at Christmas."

"You know something, Molly? Getting means giving. You don't have to do that."

"Pauline, your son always sends you money at Christmas and on your birthday. Aren't you lucky?"

"But when they come to visit me, my God! You cannot imagine how much work I have to do for them. The grandchildren behave like hooligans. You are lucky not to have to put up with all of those. Then she phoned Vera who had never married. "Your cousins got good souls to remember you every Christmas."

"Then I have to send them something back. You are lucky. Remember, Molly, not getting means no giving."

Molly understood that they were trying their best to be nice to her. But she did not feel happy or lucky either. She stood up, looked out through the window, and then opened her secret biscuit tin to see how much money she had saved so far. She had one cherished dream – a two-week cruise on a luxury liner, from port to port, place to place. A lady in leisure for two weeks. After she finished counting her money, she realised that the amount she had saved was not enough. She put the tin back in the big shoe box and hid it under the bed.

But she was thinking of doing something else on her seventy-sixth birthday. It would come soon and she was thinking of doing something better.

"Pauline, you are invited to celebrate my birthday. I'm hoping to do something new."

"Ritz or Claridges?" Pauline laughed.

"32 Midway Place. Flat 3C."

"Have you won the lottery?"

"The lottery will never reach me. All my life I worked hard for everything. Still, I can invite my three best friends to my flat for a little party, can't I? My heart is set on having you three to a special lunch at my place. I hope you will not say no to my invitation."

"Of course not. We will definitely come to your Midway Place."

"I will cook lunch for you three. After lunch we can go to play bingo."

"Brilliant idea!"

"If your heart is set darling, how can we unset it?" Vera and Ruth replied, giggling joyfully.

"So it's settled then."

"Yes. See you, darling."

"See you, love."

Special lunch means special presents, she thought. Or maybe she was really bored with crisps and peanuts.

She tore off a page from the exercise book in which she scribbled and wrote her accounts. One kilo of Basmati rice and peas for peas pillau. Six eggs for egg supreme (which she had learned from Nazia at school but never cooked), one frozen chicken for a roast. Some stuffing for the roast. For after, a tin of fruit salad and fresh cream, a bottle of Cava wine to wash down lunch nicely (she could pour that precious Cava in her crystal wine glasses which she had bought at a sale and never used them) and then something for salad and French salad dressing. For peas pillau, butter or ghee and some garam masala. When she added them all up, it was a big amount. She was feeling thirsty after adding and made herself a cup of tea. "No way I can touch my cruise money!" Her hands started to shake even thinking of it. "No way". "But I cannot cancel the party now". She muttered to herself, I have to do it somehow. She felt dizzy, but soon she shrugged it all off and said dreamily again, "I cannot let my friends down. I have to do it."

The day before her birthday, Molly went out shopping. She was wearing baggy trousers, a floral top and a massive raincoat. No one knew when it might start to rain. And a sunshine bright hat to look smart, bubbly and breezy. A small, wheeled shopping trolley was walking with her too. She looked really joyful. A daily newspaper in her trolley and some free magazines too. She was on her way to shop for her party. She chose a busy supermarket. Now and again she shopped here. The salesgirl smiled at her, even the store manager. They all liked her bubbly personality.

Everyone was busy buying and queuing up at the checkout. Some little children holding their mothers' hands, asking for sweets and stuff. Some looking for their usual items and new ones too and thinking what to buy. Molly was busy going from one aisle to another, from one shelf to another. The trolley was going with her with the *Daily Mirror* and free magazines inside. No one had any interest to see what she was picking and choosing.

Suddenly, there was a heavy sound of something falling down. The relaxed floor detective, having an ice-cold Coca Cola on a hot summer's day and thinking the cameras were doing his job, came running. Some others as well who had heard the sound. Molly was lying flat on her back. Her eyes were shut and it seemed she was unconscious. A doctor, who was busy shopping for his family, came rushing up. After checking her pulse and noting her other symptoms, he became very serious.

"Is she unconscious? What is the reason? Heart failure? High blood pressure? Exhaustion?" The crowd asked him all sorts of questions.

The doctor stood up, looking perplexed, shaking his head in bewilderment.

"Why is she unconscious?"

He replied after a little while, "She is dead."

"Dead? What's the reason?"

"Hypothermia."

"What? Hypothermia in this hot weather? How come?"

It seemed the doctor was reluctant to reply. Someone called an ambulance.

Molly's big pockets were full of groceries. The Cava bottle was in the inside pocket of her raincoat; the salad items, egg box etc. were in the various pockets of her trousers and coat. But those items were not the reason for her hypothermia. It was the big, frozen chicken sitting under her breezy, big, bright hat that had caused her body temperature to fall down so much that she got hypothermia – the condition some old people in Britain get in freezing cold weather. She thought she could get away without paying for her groceries. The cameras and the floor detective might not suspect anything if she kept on doing two potatoes in the shopping basket and the rest in her various pockets . Not just potatoes but the other items too. The whole frozen chicken under her big hat was apparently sitting quite safely there. She wanted to buy a tin of good fruit cocktail but, before sending the tin to a pocket of her trousers, poor Molly collapsed. The innocent frozen chicken was not that innocent after all! Poor Molly never thought of that. She was undertaking this sort of adventure for the first time, and she had stayed awake all night planning, How can I do it perfectly? But that blasted frozen chicken let her down badly.

Her only son James came from South Africa for the funeral. When everything was over, he went through his mother's possessions. No gold bangles and necklaces or earrings anywhere. After a long and hard search, he found the biscuit tin in a big shoe-box under the bed with five hundred and fifty-five pounds and ninety-nine pence to be precise. Molly's dream – to be a lady of leisure for two weeks in a large liner, cruising from coast to coast, from place to place – never got the wings to fly.

"Hello, Susan, do you know what my mum has left for her only son? She's been a stingy woman all her life. If I tell you the amount, you will laugh your head off."

So he told her the amount.

Susan from Johannesburg did laugh her head off.

Translated by Saleha Chowdhury

A pretty woman in an office

As she prepares to leave home, Mostafa says, "Piyali, take an umbrella. It's raining."

She will walk five minutes to the bus stop. Then she will get on the train and after that she will have to walk another five minutes to reach her office. It is a business firm. The owner is a Gujarati, Chandrakanta Patel. Piyali does the tasks of a secretary, a filing clerk, a receptionist and sometimes even the duties of a helper or an assistant. Another extra duty is of making tea or coffee. She performs all her work with care. Her main responsibility is to receive orders on the phone and send things accordingly to the right places. Piyali is one of the numerous working women of London.

"I have it in my bag," Piyali replies to her husband. She peeps in from the doorway and says, "Is there any harm in getting a little wet? It's summer!"

"Aha! That's why you're wearing the sky-blue chiffon shari. The cardigan is in the big bag and you haven't yet put that on. If you get soaked now, you'll look like a painting from Ajanta. I heard that your boss, Chandrakanta Patel, is a carnivore."

Piyali frowns at him. "And what are you? Swami Narayan's follower – a pure vegetarian?"

"No, I am not. But I get limited supplies. Am I as lucky as your Chandrakanta Patel? My office sometimes feels like a synagogue or a chapel. I have only two female colleagues. You cannot guess one's age – she is almost seventy. And the other one weighs twelve and a half stone. So . . . ."

"You don't have the luck to nibble on the side isnt it?"

"Not at all. I only have this chunk of flesh standing in front of me. At times she is pure protein and some other times she is not . . . ."

"Stop talking rubbish, will you?" Piyali knows her husband very well. He can win with his witty remarks all the time. But in reality, he is docile and good-natured. She says, "Do you think that the Ajanta painting doesn't know how to protect herself?"

"Okay, I agree that you do. But why should you get wet?"

"Do you know how old I am?" Piyali unfurls the umbrella.

"Yes, you'll be reaching the age of my grandmother very soon. But Piya, Piya, Piya . . . your dangerous curves don't have the slightest sign of my grandma."

"I have a university-going son."

"But you're still very attractive."

"Why don't you spit it out? You want me to leave that carnivore Chandrakanta Patel's office and get some other job."

"But, just now, you said that you know the techniques of self-defence like a karate specialist."

"Issh! I'm late already. We have a meeting today, so I'll be home late."

"See you, Piyali."

"See you, Mostafa." She unfolds the umbrella and walks to the main road. The sky is overshadowed with dark clouds.

Some heavy raindrops have wet her. Entering the ladies' room she observes herself in the mirror. She dabs some compact powder on her nose and darkens the *kajal* lining her eyes. She is wearing a quarter-sleeve blouse and a chiffon shari. She lets the shari face sunlight once or twice a week in summer. Usually she comes to the office in trousers and tops, salwar-kameezes or long skirts and T- shirt. Mostafa had made Piyari Ali change her name on the first night of their wedding.

"What an ancient name! My wife can't have such an old-fashioned name. As Bhabatarini became Mrinalini, I turn Piyari into Piyali."

Like her name, she also has a soft and tender diffidence in her nature that attracts everyone. Three voluptuous and glamorous girls work in this office under the supervision of Chandrakanta Patel. Meaty and Musty are in charge of supplying orders to houses. They also deliver singing messages to people. Hot and sizzling, Emily's attractive bosom can easily make her a page 3 girl of the *Sun*. There are also Bhanu from Mauritius and Priyanka from Goa in the office.

Mr. Patel has lunch with all of them and spends special time with Priyanka. She is not like a helpless doe. Instead of climbing the stairs of her career, she has leaned on Mr. Patel's shoulders to reach the second floor by elevator. No one can really say what they are up to. Both Priyanka and Mr. Patel have flats of their own. Do they have only lunch together in the office? Or is there something more to it? It would also be wrong to think that Mr. Patel has not tasted the warmth of Emily. But no one has ever seen any obscene behaviour in the rooms or corridor of the office. Piyali thinks all of this while looking at her reflection in the mirror. She sees a soft and tender woman with a lovely smile. Is a bit of narcissism natural in every human being? Maybe it is. She leaves the washroom and goes towards her table. Then she enters Mr. Patel's room.

He looks at her with hazy eyes. He is sitting drowsily at his desk. He does not seem to have any power to win over his opponents with his witty talk.

"Hello, Mr. Patel."

"Hello, Piyali."

Chandrakanta's eyes glisten. He looks at Piyali standing under the neon light. Her body wrapped in a chiffon shari, a touch of *kajal* lining her eyes, lipstick on her lips, and the twist and turns of her body.

"You look very pretty today, Piyali."

They converse mostly in English and Hindi. Mr. Patel can speak half a dozen languages.

"What would you like tea or coffee?" Usually, Emily, Bhanu and Priyanka don't get to work for another hour.

"Black coffee, Piyali – as deep and dark as your eyes. Ghastly feeling! It's because of last night's party. Yesterday was Jibon Mehta's stag night. I think you've seen him."

"Yes. Full of life, he is."

"An absolute fool! Or else, who would want to get married nowadays?"

The aroma of coffee fills the whole room.

Piyali asks, "What's wrong with getting married?"

"Slavery. I'm very allergic to that word 'faithful.' 'Faithful' is a word for dogs and cats, not for men. You're married, aren't you?"

"Yes."

"Giving your heart and life to one man – how many years have you spent like this?"

"Twenty-four years."

"Dead boring."

Piyali does not respond to his remark and arranges files.

Mr. Patel asks, "Why do you work all the time? Just take the seat in front of me and relax."

Piyali sits on the chair. The office has not come alive yet. In half an hour the scenario will change as everyone becomes busy.

"You Bengalis cook very well. Invite me to your house some day. Don't make it in weekend."

"Will you take half a day's leave?"

"I will." Some coffee spills on to the saucer – just like his untamed heart. He does not have to worry about those who come to him whenever he calls or wish to be near him willingly. Today, the charms of this lady in chiffon have shaken him up.

He says, "Have lunch with me today."

"Isn't Priyanka coming today?" asks Piyali.

"Yes, she is. Let me give you a treat for once. You've been seeing the same old face and listening to the same old voice for twenty-four years. Look at me for a change. We have been working here for two years and I haven't noticed that you are also good enough to be given a treat." Chandrakanta Patel laughs.

"Thank you. But I don't want to throw the lunch I've brought from home into the bin."

"Okay then. When are you inviting me to your home? All that stuff you cook! *Chochchori*, potato with poppy seeds, *bori*, *khichuri*, etc. I lived in Bengal in my childhood. I still remember those homely foods. Now I live on the boring meals of restaurants or take-aways."

"I'll definitely invite you." Piyali stands up.

"I'll be waiting."

Piyali gets ready to leave the room and laughs to herself as the last words of Mr. Patel echo in her mind, "Just a chaste peck, Piyali, don't be afraid."

It seems that he wanted to tell Piyali, "My lady, you're also very attractive." After that, Piyali's face loses the finishing touch of this morning's make-up. It bears strong traits of her personality. The forty-eight-year-old Piyali, who has a university-going son, wears her usual serious mask again in Chandrakanta Patel's office. Today when both of them were alone in the office, Piyali could have asked, "Who'll get the post of Dispatch Clerk?" or she could have said, "I would be delighted to have lunch with you." But Piyali did not say that. She was happy to be able to hold on to her personality.

When she again enters Mr. Patel's room to give him a file, she does not forget to wear a cardigan. But Mr. Patel is also an expert businessman. He was able to set up this business in the West End because of his brains. At the 4 o'clock tea time he acts as if nothing has happened.

"How long have you been here, Piyali?" he asks while taking the cup in his hand.

"Twenty-six years."

"Twenty-six years! And you've been working here just as a clerk?"

"I don't understand what do you mean."

"Listen, success never comes straight away. If you were a bit tactful in the morning, I would've looked into your promotion before completing my tenure in this office. An unimaginable success could have been all yours."

"Aren't you happy with my work?"

Mr. Patel laughs. "A Bengali gentleman will be sitting here in my seat in seven days. He is nearly sixty years old. A spiritual man who is into meditation and yoga. I think you'll feel safer with him." He looks into Piyali's eyes and says, "Just loosen up a bit. You don't have to be so stiff all the time."

Jibon Mehta enters the room at that moment. Mr. Patel relaxes by placing his feet on the table and takes out a bottle of wine from the bottom drawer. Priyanka walks into the room, flaunting her hair. Piyali has heard that Emily will accompany Mr. Patel to Manchester. He believes the new branch has many positions that Emily can handle well.

Piyali writes on Chandrakanta's goodbye card, "I hope you reach the sky."

He starts laughing as usual. "And I will look down at you from there."

The new boss, Subinoy Tripathi, is from Calcutta. His character is as bright as the sun. He hardly speaks any word unnecessarily. If someone asks, "Would you like to have your morning tea now?" his answer is monosyllabic: "Yes" or "No."

One day Piyali asks him while arranging his files, "Do you live here alone?"

"Yes." He looks at her beautiful face and utters a few more words, "It was too late for my own marriage after I managed to marry off my five sisters. Youth had said goodbye to me by then."

This simple statement makes Piyali feel sorry for him. All women feel a certain ache inside them without any specific reason whatsoever. He reads the *Guardian* and has lunch out of a plastic tiffin box. *Chapati* and vegetable curry are his usual lunch. Perhaps, he cooks them himself. The aroma of *panchforon* or mixed spices and onion seeds has tickled Piyali's nostrils quite a few times. What kind of woman would she be if she does not notice these things while making tea for him?

"Don't you have any of your sisters nearby?"

"They are busy with their own families. Two sisters live in Calcutta and the other three live in the US."

"Did you make those *chapatis*?"

"Yes. I learnt how to cook long time ago."

"Should I make a cup of tea for you?"

"No, get on with your work."

Still, Piyali waits a little and then leaves the room. While having lunch, she enjoys looking out of the window at the life in motion outside.

After she has finished lunch, she enters Mr. Tripathi's room. "Would you like to have a piece of *sandesh*? It's homemade."

"No, thank you, Mrs. Mostafa."

Piyali returns to her small office room. Bhanu shares this space with her but he has gone out right now. She remembers the sentence "Youth said goodbye to me when I had managed to marry off my five sisters." Some people's lives are like this.

One day Piyali asks Subinoy Tripathi as she brings his files, "Where do you live?"

"In Lewisham."

"That's near my place! I live in Heathergreen."

The next day Piyali presents herself in front of Tripathi in a chiffon shari. "The office will be closed tomorrow for stocktaking. What are your plans for tomorrow?"

Mr. Tripathi looks at the Piyali who has loosened the nuts and bolts of her life. He observes her carefully and then shifts his eyes to the paper on which he has been working.

"Could I make a suggestion?"

"What suggestion?" Mr. Tripathi answers while scribbling on the paper.

"Tomorrow is a holiday. I would like to invite you to have lunch at my place. It's a twenty-minute drive from your house."

"Is your husband's office closed tomorrow too?"

"He'll be at work. But that is no big deal. I can't invite you to the dinner as we have another programme in the evening."

Piyali's innocent face is lit up with the radiance of taking the bold step of inviting him.

"That means you are inviting me to your house when your husband will not be at home."

She does not get his insinuation at first. Gradually, her ears turn red in embarrassment when she understands. "You have the same old *chapati* and curry every day. Tomorrow you can taste something different for a change."

"I have brought up five sisters myself and married them off before any scandal could taint and tarnish their characters. They are all living happily with their husbands."

He looks at the little simple but attractive Piyali in chiffon. Piyali, who has loosened the nuts and bolts of her body before coming to Mr. Tripathi, whose face is not pink with powder anymore but has turned red like her ears instead.

"You'll get your promotion automatically," Mr. Tripathi says.

Back in her own office, Piyali sits down in her chair. She says to herself, "Are you scared of getting raped in an empty house, mister?"

She had not liked Chandrakanta. But does she likes this person, though it seems who has halos round his head . Ofcourse not.

Piyali fans herself with a thin file.

Translated by Sabreena Ahmed

Rahim and Karim

Moulana Abdul Hakim Hakimpuri had been living in the village of Hatsherpur for quite some years. Hatsherpur is a village located in the *thana* of Shariakandi, famous mainly because the *mazar* of Qudratullah Munshi is there. During his lifetime, he used to keep hundreds of jinns. He had cured thousands of people and had performed such amazing miracles that the villagers proclaimed his grave a holy shrine. This took place about fifty years ago. And perhaps it was because of this *mazar* that Moulana Hakimpuri did not want to leave. If one searches his genealogy, one will find that his paternal grandfather's paternal grandfather had come to this land from faraway Khorasan in Iran.

Moulana Hakimpuri had never married. He was an abstemious person, a Sufi. With his flowing beard and long robes, he was greeted with respect wherever he went. People kowtowed low before him in the dust. In his *khankah* there was always water from the Zamzam spring, Arabian dates, and dry fruits. Villagers would come to him to get dates sanctified by holy words. Every villager prayed that when death came, they would be able to drink Zamzam water from the moulana's hands and die listening to his recitation of holy verses. That is why when people sent for him on their deathbeds, he would rush with Zamzam water and the *Wazifa Sharif,* a selection of Quranic verses, in his hands. He would keep the last wish of those departing forever. And with a full heart, he would pray for them.

Recently, a strange disease had broken out in epidemic form at Hatsherpur. Everyone said that the disease had started from the cowshed of Kalu the dairyman. The stricken person would suffer from high fever and cramps in arms and legs. Before death came, there would be severe vomiting. Though a couple of patients recovered after eating his sanctified dates and drinking Zamzam water, the number of deaths rose to thirty-eight. No one knew the cause of the disease. No one knew who was susceptible to it. Almost every night, Moulana Hakimpuri would be called to someone's beside to give a drink of Zamzam water and to recite Quranic verses. For this reason, he remained very busy. And it was seen that most patients died at night.

"That wicked Kalu has been adding water to his milk and we are suffering."

Whether the fault was Kalu Goala's cannot be stated with any certainty. But there was no doubt that some deadly virus was rampant in the village. Even a couple of MBBS doctors could not explain the cause of the disease.

Moulana Hakimpuri said, "In the Quran it is stated that when the world becomes full of sin, Allah will send diseases like this."

"Have only the people of Hatsherpur sinned, Huzoor?" the villagers asked.

He replied, "This is the holy place where Qudratullah Munshi's *mazar* is located. It is wrong to sin here."

Kalu was forced to confess his crime and promise never to commit it again. But this was to no avail. The virulence of the disease did not abate.

One night a call came for Moulana Hakimpuri from Miyajan Mridha, whose wife, Amina Begum, was very ill. He picked up a bottle of Zamzam water and the *Wazifa Sharif.* Qudratullah Munshi used to have a horse to take him wherever he needed to go. If Moulana Hakimpuri had to travel some distance, he would go by rickshaw van. But he decided that he would walk to Amina Begum's place. Miyajan Mridha was the most important person of Hatsherpur village. He possessed about a hundred *bighas* of land. But, despite his wealth, he had just one wife. Amina Begum had been blessed with seven children. Moulana Hakimpuri had been to Amina Begum's place before as well, to attend religious ceremonies, to circumcise her sons, to conduct *milads*. He had been there several times. Miyajan Mridha had a cluster of four tin-roofed houses. The courtyard was huge – almost a field. He had a cowshed and a *dhenki* shed, where paddy was husked. He had a plastered water trough and a tubewell. One modern bathroom. Amina Begum was a plump, placid woman. A quiet person, she didn't talk much. She was an excellent cook. The person who had once eaten *polao* cooked by her would never forget the taste. Of course, he too would never forget. Other people's *polaos* were never as fragrant.

Perhaps with these thoughts in mind, he quickened his steps. Electricity had come to the house. But power cuts were frequent. A huge, oil-burning lamp had been placed near Amina Begum's bed. Moulana Hakimpuri pulled up a chair and sat next to it. The children were all asleep. Only two daughters were continually wiping their eyes. Amina Begum would be thirty-eight at the most.

Looking at Amina Begum, Moulana Hakimpuri realised that Azrael, the angel of death, was not too far away. Perhaps his overtime had already started. He would seize one life and immediately go on to seize another.

Moulana Hakimpuri said, "Ma, Amina Begum, take Allah's name."

Amina Begum did not reply. She had no power of speech left. Was this the same Amina Begum who used to be so plump and fair? Now she was just a skeleton with some flesh sticking to her bones. Her face had shriveled up to such an extent that she was almost unrecognisable. Her hair was matted, like string. Someone had tried to cover her head, but the veil had fallen away to reveal her hair. Patients suffering from this disease could not bear to wear any clothes.

Moulana Hakimpuri sprinkled some Zamzam water on her lips. Then he said, "Ma, try and say *La illaha illallah mohammadar rasulallah.*" The attempt was futile. Amina Begum could neither hear nor speak. She had lost her senses.

Moulana Hakimpuri prayed aloud and then blew into Amina Begum's ears so that the blessing of the prayer could enter her body. He wrote something on her forehead. He realised that Azrael had finished his work with Amina Begum and proceeded elsewhere to take another soul. Still, Amina Begum had died peacefully.

The cry of wailing arose in the house. Those who had been sleeping awoke. Amina Begum's husband wiped his eyes on his sleeves several times. Yes, his wife had truly been a good woman. She had been married at eighteen. She had brightened Miyajan Mridha's household for twenty years; she had brightened the village with her beauty and goodness. Now she had gone to light up Paradise. Miyajan Mridha had married her because she had been a wonderful girl. He had been twenty-four at the time. He had heard that she had many suitors. One of them, frustrated in his suit, had left the country.

If he spoke about this to Amina Begum, she would leave the room without saying anything.

Thinking that it was a woman's modesty that affected his wife, Miyajan Mridha did not pursue the matter. Now this woman was dead. Now she would no longer be able to provide the happiness that she had all these years. Every time Miyajan Mridha thought of this, he had to wipe his eyes with his sleeve.

"Why are you crying, Baap? The lucky man's wife passes away before him." These words of an aunt's angered him, but then he calmed down. "So many proposals will start coming for you from tomorrow. How can the man who possesses a hundred *bighas* of land not find a wife?"

Hakimpuri grieved at the passing of Amina Begum. No one could make *murgi musallam* or roast chiken like she could. She would stuff the inside cavity of the chicken with raisins and others. He was a little perturbed that he was thinking of food at this sad moment. But he consoled himself that it was only in his thoughts. No one else knew what he was thinking. So, reciting prayers loudly, he returned home.

It was late at night. The entire village was asleep. No news had come to him that night. No one had called for him either. He was sleeping soundly. Suddenly at about two in the morning, he heard someone knocking at the door. Someone was rattling the iron rings loudly. He tried to ignore the knocking at first, but could not continue to do so. He had to get up finally.

He opened the door and stepped outside. The moonlight was still lighting up the place.

A very tall man said, "You have to come at once, Hakimpuri Saheb."

"How far? To whose house?"

The man did not reply to the question, but said, "Come with me, Huzoor. You have to give water on which holy verses have been recited to someone."

Moulana Hakimpuri thought that he had never seen the man before. As far as he knew, there was no one in the village as tall as the stranger. But the man's accent belonged to the village.

He asked, "Where must I go?"

"Come with me, Huzoor." The man seemed to be standing some distance away. Not close. And it wasn't as if he was speaking either. But Moulana Hakimpuri could understand the man.

"Do you belong to Hatsherpur?"

"Yes, Huzoor. Take Zamzam water and the *Wazifa Sharif* and follow me."

Moulana Hakimpuri took a bottle of Zamzam water and the *Wazifa Sharif* and followed the man. When others called him, they would take these things from his hands. He would walk with his hands free. But the tall man did not take anything from him. It appeared as if he was walking on air. Hakimpuri could not understand why the man was not walking beside him. Occasionally, Hakimpuri asked, "Can you hear me? How much farther is the place where you are taking me?"

"Just ahead. There." The man gestured towards the spot.

Hatsherpur was a small village. Hakimpuri knew all the houses in it. Finally, they stopped in front of a brick house. The house was famous as the house of Hashem Kabiraj. No one lived there anymore. However, occasionally someone would come, stay for a short while, then leave. Hashem Kabiraj had passed away quite some years ago. The house was on the bank of the same Jamuna river that had eroded its banks and reduced the size of the village. The river could draw the house down at any moment. When the house had been built, the river was at some distance. Now it had come close. There were no embankments at this spot. The bank could collapse at any moment.

The tall man opened the door of the house. Then he said, "Please go upstairs."

On the upper storey there was only one room. Hashem Kabiraj could not complete the upper floor. As no one stayed in the house, there was no electricity. At the top of the stairs, a clay lamp was burning, providing a dim light. The stairs were dirty, with clusters of cobwebs everywhere. The place had not been swept for ages.

Moulana Hakimpuri somehow managed to make his way upstairs. Then he asked, "You there – where am I supposed to go?"

Looking around, he saw that the tall man was nowhere to be seen.

A faint light filtered through from the room. Moulana Hakimpuri was not easily frightened. Thanks to Almighty Allah, no ghosts, spirits, jinns or fairies could ever harm him. He recited a prayer and blew upon his chest. Then, with the bottle of Zamzam water in one hand and the *Wazifa Sharif* in the other, he entered the room.

A man was lying down on a bed. He was covered neck down. Only his head was visible. In the epidemic which was sweeping through the village, no affected person could bear to wear clothes. But this man was covered with a sheet. On the window sill, a lamp was burning. In its light, he could make out that the man was still alive.

Moulana Hakimpuri sat down beside the man.

Looking at the man, Moulana Hakimpuri asked, "Can you hear me?"

A bat had got stuck in the room. It flew from one side of the room to the other, futilely trying to escape. Was it a bat or a vampire?

Moulana Hakimpuri enquired again, "Can you hear me?"

The man answered, "Yes."

Moulana Hakimpuri asked, "How are you?"

"Not well. I am going to die," the man said faintly, struggling to say the words.

"What is wrong with you?"

"The doctor says cancer. I think he's right."

"Cancer?" Moulana Hakimpuri was startled. "If you have cancer, why are you here? Why didn't you go to Dhaka or to some other place?"

"No. They have given up."

"But then, why here and alone?"

"I belong to this house."

"Oh. You have no one else?"

"I do. But I have not informed any of them. They would not be happy to know about me. I am a thief, a robber."

"No, no. Don't speak like that. You are one of Allah's creatures."

The man remained silent for some time.

"Huzoor, about twenty years ago, I left the village. The country."

"Why?"

"I had been badly hurt, Huzoor."

"After that?"

"After that, Huzoor, I travelled to many countries. I supported myself through petty thieving. When I left, my friend Karim too left the village with me."

"Karim?"

"Yes, Huzoor, my close friend."

"Why did you resort to thieving?"

"My having led a good life had not helped. I could not marry the woman I wanted to. That was the cause of my bitterness."

"Where did you go finally?"

"Makkah. It is difficult to steal there. You perhaps know that if they catch a thief there, they cut off his hand. That is why we would steal money from hajjis. There are a lot of foolish pilgrims. It was convenient."

Moulana Hakimpuri listened stupefied to this strange tale. This man robbed hajjis. Shame! How could he pray for this man and give him Zamzam water? Suddenly he remembered the saying, "Hate the sin, not the sinner. You do not know the man's soul". That was what his father used to say. He sat up straight again. The bat flew around once more, then quietly clung to one spot. The room was full of old cobwebs.

"How long have you been here?"

"Three days."

"Who looked after you these three days?"

"No one. At every moment I thought I was about to die. But you can see I am not dead yet."

"I can." After a pause Moulana Hakimpuri said, "Where is your friend, Karim?"

"Inside the desert."

"Meaning?"

"He passed away there."

"How?"

"Smallpox."

After a long pause, the man said, "I brought a religious man to him and made him say the *kalma*. Made him do the *taoba*, repent his sins. Arranged to give him Zamzam water. I said, 'You stayed with me.

113

You cannot leave me. I was not supposed to be a thief today, neither were you. I am trying to help your soul in its departing moment.' In gratitude, he almost wept, 'One day I shall repay you for this kind deed.'

"'You are dying,' I said 'How will you repay me?'

"He said, 'You will know when I do.'"

It was very late. Rahim had grown tired. Perhaps he would pass away now.

Moulana Hakimpuri said, "You must recite the *taoba* now."

Rahim seemed to grow a little happier at these words. Then he said, "Tell me, Huzoor, how did you know I was here?"

"Why? A man fetched me."

"A man? Which man?" In his surprise, he wanted to sit up. But he fell back.

Again he said, "Which man? I didn't tell anyone I was here. Why was it necessary to tell anyone? I have come to my village to die. The village I had left twenty years ago. I had suffered greatly that day." The suffering seemed to be there still, the way he clutched his chest.

Recovering some strength in his voice, he asked, "But which man called you here?"

"I don't know his name. But he was about six feet two inches tall. Like a palmyra palm."

"Karim! Karim brought you here? I understand I do not have long now. Yes, Huzoor, administer the *taoba*. Help me to recite my prayers. Do all that is necessary to ease my soul." As he spoke, Rahim's eyes closed.

The Zamzam water had gone down his throat. The words of the holy *kalma* had entered his ears. And a lot of other prayers. He had said the *taoba* in his full senses. The thief's soul would now depart in peace.

Moulana Hakimpuri recited the holy verses aloud. The cobwebs tore apart at the resounding voice. He sweated as he continued to recite the verses. In the light of the lamp, he realised that Rahim had closed his eyes forever. The door of the room burst open. The bat flew straight out of the doorway.

Moulana Hakimpuri glanced in the direction of the door. A blaze of light was coming from the doorway. And, standing in that light, was a figure. He recognised the person. It was Amina Begum, her arms extended.

She was just eighteen. Moulana Hakimpuri heard her sweet voice saying, "Come. Let us go now, you and I."

Outside the window, Moulana Hakimpuri could see the dawn sky. He could hear the cries of countless birds.

Translated By Niaz Zaman

Father and They

Father is reading in the study. Rumki brushes aside the curtain and peeps in. He is absorbed in a book. The coffee cup on the side table is empty. A burning cigarette butt is lying there in the ashtray. Father smokes four to five cigarettes a day. He smokes a cigarette after breakfast in the morning, after lunch, after tea in the afternoon, and the last one after having dinner . Father never smokes more than that. Rumki cannot make up her mind if she should enter the study or not. Perhaps Father has noticed that she is standing here. He does not take his eyes off the book as he asks: "Rumki, do you want to say something?"

Rumki enters the room. She is a smart and sophisticated woman. She is wearing trousers and a T-shirt with the motif of a cat. Her hair is drawn back and tied up high above the nape of her neck. There is a touch of *kajal* in her eyes and perhaps a smidgen of cream on her face – that's it. She looks beautiful – unsurpassable! Rumki is twenty-two . A wonderful twenty-two unlike the twenty-four of Rumki's mother, who had been tired, exhausted and weak because of a disease in her uterus.

Rumki pulls up a chair beside her father. Father places a bookmark in the book he is reading and looks at Rumki.

"What's the matter, Rumki?"

Rumki does not speak.

Father asks, "How is your thesis progressing?"

"Three more months," answers Rumki. Her father is happy to hear this. After finishing her honours in biology, Rumki started writing her thesis on a difficult subject. Only Rumki and her father live in this house. Her mother passed away when Rumki was sixteen.

Looking at Rumki's face, her father realises that she has come to him with a special purpose.

"You will like him this time."

"Who's he?"

"He is from Uttar Pradesh. Abinish."

"What does he do?" Father is not bothered about where someone is from. He is interested in the man's speech, manners and behaviour. He sees if he is intelligent or not. And surely the husband of his daughter has to be courteous and gentle. Father had rejected some of the men before. He had been displeased with their talk. Some had no ambition in life and some others were just blockheads! But Rumki will not marry without her father's consent. Yes, Rumki will marry, and her father has given her permission to search for a bridegroom. He wants Rumki to get married as soon as she has finished her thesis. But the bridegroom has to fulfil all the criteria given by him, he has to meet his approval. This is an unwritten agreement between Father and Rumki.

Rumki grew up and studied in Britain. Now she is writing her thesis. Maybe she will get a well-paid job. Father told her to get married before starting work. He had said, "Search for the man you like. But bring him to me once."

The suitors were rejected. Father did not like the first one's philosophy of life.

He asked, "What is the definition of life?"

The boy answered, "Speed." He thought that he had given an appropriate, intellectual answer.

But Rumki's father took a little time and said, "Do you know that sometimes life has to learn to take a break? Be still to see own reflection."

The boy searched for another intellectual answer. Rumki's father inquired about his family. The family background was not very pleasant. His father was a wholesale rice trader in Dhaka. Rumki was ready to give the boy two extra points for his honesty, but not her father.

The next one was so dull-headed that Father bade him goodbye after talking for only five minutes.

He asked, "What is love?" The boy started on such a long lecture that Rumki's father grew annoyed and said, "Can't you just say it concisely? Something like, 'Man's love is of man's life a thing apart. 'Tis woman's whole existence.'"

The boy wanted to write a draft of his long lecture.

Rumki's father said, "You may go, but do have a cup of tea before leaving."

Even though the third one was a computer wizard, he made Rumki's father angry by confessing that he did not like reading books.

"How will you become a human being if you don't read books?" Rumki's father asked him.

"What do you think I am?"

"Human."

"Then?"

"I have to think of Rumki's future. That responsibility is mine. I want a human being for her, a thoughtful human being who has imagination. Someone who won't buy things according to a shopping list. Someone capable of thinking beyond the list. And his list can be enriched through reading – not reading for academic purposes, but reading for himself."

"I'll not have a shopping list but I'll buy whatever I like."

"That's great. But indiscipline makes one's life imbalanced." Rumki's father would have liked him if his answers had been pleasing. But he could not say, "You may leave" to him at first sight as he seemed to be pretty solid. That is why the long interview.

"But if you do not read books, you'll never know that there is a rule even in buying whatever you like. And also, you'll not realise that there is a delight in disorder."

"Do you want a book or a man?"

"Beg your pardon?" What is this man saying? "Do you want a book or a man?"

"A man who reads books is a complete human being." Rumki's father got absorbed in his book and said, "There is a huge difference between your wavelength and Rumki's."

In fact, the difference was between her father and him.

"We do get along."

"Maybe. But – you may go." Rumki's father did not want to prolong the conversation. From his attitude it seemed that all these men had come for job interviews. His speech was peppered with comments such as "You may go," "That's enough," "Your answer is incorrect," "More precise and brief."

Rumki had never said a word about this. If her father rejected one candidate, Rumki brought the next one.

"You know something? You're a very possessive father." The computer wizard, the non-book-lover, wanted to say something very harsh. He looked at the face of Rumki's father angrily.

"Yes I know." Saying this, Rumki's father looked indifferently out of the window. Within five minutes of the young man's departure, he took up the book in his hand again.

"You are not fated to get married. I didn't come to be interviewed by your father."

"I can't do anything. I am helpless if Father is not happy." Then Rumki moved the curtain aside and said exactly in her father's tone, "I wish you best of luck."

"Damn you and your dad. Damn your best of luck."

That was it. This one was dismissed as well. Thank heavens that all of them were Rumki's friends, classmates, in fact. Or else Rumki would have died of burning heartache.

After all of them had left, Rumki stood in front of her father with a smile on her face. "I'm bringing someone more. You will definitely like him."

Rumki's father has retired from an executive post in a multi-national company. He reads books and sometimes plays golf.

Rumki says, "Baba, you've been alone all your life."

"Your mother and I were not compatible. I am better off without her. I am selecting grooms for you so that you don't feel as she used to. But the best gift of my marriage is you." Saying this, father goes back to his book.

"Having the disease was not mother's fault, Baba," Rumki says to her father.

"But, before that? I don't think I have to discuss our conjugal life with you."

"Do you think you are perfect?"

"Almost. But only if I . . . ." Rumki's father does not continue.

Rumki says, "I won't do anything against your will, Baba."

No, Rumki will not get involved in a relationship. Rumki will marry a man approved by her father. Her father has sacrificed everything in his life for Rumki's sake. She will make him happy in return – this is her decision, a contract. Her father also expects that from her. He seems to think that Rumki is almost perfect as well.

When Rumki was a rippling eighteen, a boy popped up in front of her out of the blue and then sank like a stone. He created a storm inside Rumki. The boy did not like Rumki's father.

He said, "A woman can have only one man in her life at a time, not two. I can't think of fighting a duel with your father."

Rumki watched him go away. She did not say anything.

Rumki is as bright as the stars!

Rumki asks her father, "What will you hold on to if I go away?"

"Books," is her father's answer. Books are everything to him.

"That's imperfection"

"That's why I said 'almost.'" Rumki's father laughs. Then he asks about Abinish, "What does Abinish do?"

"A job."

"What kind of job?"

"Executive post in a bank. You'll like him. I met him while withdrawing the scholarship money for my thesis. I told him that only pleasing me wouldn't do. He had to please you as well."

"Did you invite him to come?"

"Should I?"

"Of course."

Rumki says politely -"Baba may I take bit of rest after this? I mean if you dont like him!"

"Yes, ofcourse!"

Abinish will come on Sunday. Abinish Iyer. He is the son of a professor from Uttar Pradesh.

"I might have to live in India for some time after the marriage."

"That's not a problem."

So the man Rumki has chosen has promised to come on Sunday. Father and daughter lay the table together.

Plates, forks, teaspoons, dessert spoons, napkins.

A bottle of red wine.

A bottle of water.

A large Ikebana arrangement of red carnations and green leaves.

The table glows with some other things. It has been covered with a lace tablecloth. There are placemats on the table, set with shining Wedgewood plates.

"Baba, please remember" says Rumki again "If you don't like him, I want to take a break for some time in this matter. I want to do some other work. After that we can resume this game of ours again."

"What other work?"

"I want to do some research on the large iguanas on the Galapagos Islands, the successors of the dinosaurs. I have been thinking about it for quite some time."

"Will you go there alone?"

"What's the harm if I have to?"

"Well, don't forget to take books with you. You'll have your own time after your biology research. You can read books. But I have a feeling from what you have said that I might like Abinish."

He likes the touch of the boy's hand as he shakes hands with him. It is neither very soft nor too rough. He has sparkling, intelligent eyes. He has great hair. Thirty years of age. An attractive way of talking. Rumki's father is pleased to note that he has goals. Even his fashionable get-up is nice. Rumki's father and Abinish exchange views on different topics. Their opinions match perfectly on various issues.

Rumki thinks, "What a surprise! Has this man done research on Baba before coming here?"

The two men empty one wine glass each and then take another. Both of them light a cigarette after their meal. Father smiles meekly. It is clear that Rumki will get married within the next three months, the day after submitting her thesis. Rumki does not speak much. She merely looks at the two men sitting with her. She listens to their conversation. The way the man lifts a spoon to his lips is also very interesting to watch. Most Asian men do not know how to use different cutlery. They eat dessert with teaspoons instead of dessert forks. While listening to their conversation and watching her father's bright smile, Rumki picks up a fork that has fallen and puts it back on the table. The fruit cocktail ends. They will go to the living room to have coffee.

Abinish does not notice that his jacket is pinned to the tablecloth. The expected incident takes place. Everything on the table drops to the floor with the tablecloth. How did this happen at the last moment? It takes time to put everything back in order.

Rumki's father and Abinish sip their tea gravely. Their conversation on Camus, Sartre, etc., does not go very far. Not even on Paul Valery or Heinrich Heine, or Baba's Chandi Das and his poetry.

Abinish stands up. How can this be? The colour of his jacket is the same as Rumki's father's. And the design on his tie – her father has one exactly like that!

"Good night."

"Good night," Rumki's father replies, looking at Abinish's jacket. He looks at Abinish's shoes.

"What size do you wear?"

"Seven-and-a-half."

"That 'half' is where we don't match. I'm size eight," says Rumki's father.

"It depends on the shoe company."

"I see." Rumki's father seems to be thinking of something.

After that father retires for the night, Rumki goes to his room and sits down.

"What a day, Baba! He pulled down the tablecloth with everything on the table while getting up. How clumsy of him!" says Rumki.

"But he is so much like me. How could it have happened?"

"Clumsy. He made a mess."

Rumki's father looks at her face and says, "What happened with the tablecloth was an accident. It could have happened with me also. Do you have to take it so seriously, Rumki?"

"What are you saying?" replies Rumki.

"Rumki, I am ready to excuse this accident."

"What do you mean?"

"You have my blessings to marry him."

Rumki looks at her father coldly. She says firmly, "How can I marry such a clumsy person, Baba? It's worse than slurping tea or soup. Suppose we get married, and we go to a party and the same thing happens? What then? You are not thinking about me."

Her father does not say anything. He is a rational man.

Rumki gets up and goes to her room.

Rumki did not marry a man wearing shoes, a jacket and a tie like her father. She had pinned the man's jacket to the tablecloth when she was picking up the fork from underneath the table. Why?

When Rumki was eighteen, a beautiful murmuring brook entered her life. He did not like her father. He said that, in a woman's life, one man was enough. Now he is doing some research on the Galapagos Islands, in a house with a thatched roof. There would be no other man to stand as a wall between them. There was no dining table there, no different types of tableware, no serviettes, no napkins folded in different ways, no flowers arranged Ikebana style. Rumki would cook on a simple fire stove. She would sometimes have to eat termites and ant eggs and leaves of trees. The young man had not thought of any woman after Rumki. And Rumki? Weren't six years long enough for Rumki to realise the truth? Her heart? As her father always says, "After all, love is a woman's whole existence."

Translated by Sabreena Ahmed

One Kilogram of Holy Meat

It was about time to return to London, after my annual six weeks' summer holiday in Bangladesh. All the packaging and other bits had been done, and I was looking at my two travelling suitcases. Three new *jamdani* sharis which I got this morning as gifts were lying on the floor. I wondered how to put these three sharis in my suitcases which were overflowing already. I always carry two suitcases. One for my personal belongings and the other for gifts, medicines, etc. Sabrina had asked me to get some books from Dhaka. I could not say "No" to her as she was one of my best friends. The books with other gifts for people in London were fully packed too. My relatives and friends loved to send gifts from Dhaka for their respective favourites, so I always had some extra luggage when I returned to London. Though in London there were all sorts of Indian sweetmeat shops, they never listened to me and always gave me something for their friends and relatives. I also sometimes got containers full of hilsa and koi fish as well as other half-cooked foods.

"Look, there's no need to send fish. You probably don't know that we get the biggest hilsa and koi in the Bangladeshi shops in London and also in other towns. They are bigger and more beautiful than you will ever find in Dhaka markets. As you know, those fish travel all over the world to catch pounds, dollars, yens for clever expatriate greengrocers."

But who's going to listen? So my other suitcase was packed with fish, sweetmeats, green vegetables (however, when those green vegetables reach London, they do not look so green after all), honey, pickles, ghee, etc. I was thinking hard where to put those three sharis. I was allowed seven kilos in my hand luggage. I thought that was the only place I could squeeze in those three new sharis. My hand luggage carried some travelling books, Sudoku, crossword puzzles, some useful medicines, one set of clothes and three fresh knickers. Sometimes the airplane loo was filthy; clothes got soiled and messy. Fresh knickers made me feel good. A jotter pad and a pen came in handy too, so I carried them as well.

When I was thinking about how to sort my luggage, the phone started to ring.

"Hello."

"Hello, Apu. It's Reenee."

"How are you, my dear? You never came to see me in six weeks. Is everything all right with you?"

"My family is suffering from flu. One person gets better then someone else gets it. It's a kind of peculiar virus they say. I've just recovered from it and was wondering whether you were still in Dhaka or had gone back to London."

"I'm still here but am leaving for London tonight."

"When do you think you will leave home to go to the airport?"

"The plane will depart at ten, so I should leave home about seven, I guess."

"Good! Then I can come to meet you."

"Okay," I said.

"But, Apu, please do me a favour."

"What's the favour? Please do not ask me to carry some presents for your sister Rosie and her family. No room for that. Moreover, Rosie lives in Leeds and I live in London. It's not convenient, you see."

"Please, Apu, it's not much. Just a kilo of *Qurbani* meat. We slaughtered Shurovi this year, and you probably know that Shurovi was Rosie's favourite cow. She could not make it here for Eid-ul-Adha and it's a golden opportunity to send Rosie some half-cooked meat with you. Oh, Apu, she would be so pleased."

"Are you suggesting that I take the meat to London and then go to Leeds to deliver it?"

"You don't have to go. Her husband, Naim, is coming to London soon. You can give the meat to him. You can keep it in your deep fridge for the time being."

"We get all sorts of beef in London, Reenee. From Jersey and Devon cattle. The best sirloin. From European, Australian, American cattle. I saw a shop in Surbiton with a sign saying 'We sell all sorts of colonial meat.' What then is the point of sending meat to London?"

"But this is *Qurbani* meat, Apu, holy meat. Not just a kilo of ordinary meat. In the name of Allah, we slaughter animals and that meat is supposed to be really holy." Reenee tried to explain to me what she meant by holy meat.

"Look, Reenee, though by choice I'm a vegetarian, I know what *Qurbani* meat means. But how come you slaughtered Shurovi? How on earth could you slaughter her? We saw her last year in your farmhouse. Shurovi was so sweet, cute and docile that I fell in love with her."

"This time of the year Allah wants something which is very dear to us. To please Allah, Prophet Ibrahim wanted to slaughter his dear son Ismail. But Allah stopped him and asked him to slaughter a *dumba* instead. A *dumba* is nothing but a special, fat-tailed sheep. Our Prophet Mohammed included this ritual in his doctrine, so we have to do it, Apu, on Eid-ul-Adha."

"Do I need this religious lecture? I know the history and geography of it and more."

"I know you do not like slaughtering animals. But the rest of the Muslim world observes this ritual, Apu."

"I sacrifice some of my savings and distribute that money to the poor. My idea of sacrifice is not the same as yours. My savings are very dear to me. They are my friend for rainy days, so I sacrifice some of that, Reenee. It says in the Quran `sacrifice'! And I do just that – sacrifice my money instead."

"The whole Muslim world does as our Prophet says."

"That makes our Allah really bloodthirsty, don't you think? Is He sitting up there, waiting to drink animal blood each year – gallons upon gallons?"

"Oh, Apu, this is not the time to argue about that. I know you have your reason for not doing what we do, but please, Apu, please take one kilo of meat for me."

I looked at the suitcases, overflowing and overburdened with stuff. There was no place for a needle to squeeze in there.

But Reenee almost cried and begged me to take a portion of Shurovi for Rosie.

"Make a good packet of that holy meat of yours. Put it in a tight plastic container, then put that into another carrier bag, and tie it well. I do not want my clothes getting holier by the minute from Shurovi's juices. Dear Allah, help me!"

"I will do just that, Apu."

Reenee lived in Pubail, about thirty kilometres from Dhaka. She had a farmhouse with some animals, gardens, etc. They loved to live like the people in *Good Life*. *Good Life* was a popular serial on London television and she had liked that serial very much and started to live in the *Good Life* style. Overjoyed, Reenee hired an auto rickshaw, promising him a handsome fare for a round-trip journey and fifteen minutes' waiting time.

The *jamdanis* were not going with me then, I thought. I could keep those in my wardrobe in Dhaka and wear them the next time I came. A sort of solution was working in my head. No way I could put that meat in my hand luggage. Food is prohibited in hand luggage.

Reenee came. Gave me that special packet of holy meat with a million thanks and a huge hug. Then she rushed home as her house was infested with some unknown flu virus.

"How many kilos of `good deeds' for Allah are going with one kilo of holy meat, Renee?"

"Only Allah can tell!" Reenee went out like a gust of stormy wind. She was always like that.

After returning to London, I put the sacrificial meat in my deep fridge and got on with my life. One of my colleagues at school had left the school to be a check-out girl in a supermarket and was feeling very happy about it. "I have had enough, no more of that!" she declared just before the summer holidays. I thought my head teacher would probably ask me to take that class. I had always wanted to leave my "honourable" teaching profession and was even willing to sweep the streets to earn some money instead. But I could not make up my mind. The reason might be that there was a bit of showing off there when I told my friends and relatives back home that I was a school teacher in London. I believe everybody has a weak spot somewhere, and I was not an exception. So I was busy with planning, recording, making games, etc. for the Autumn term again.

God! how those hooligans in sixth form could make someone so miserable. I always preferred Nursery but that was not always given to me.

I had to phone Rosie to tell her, "Rosie, the holy meat is here. Please come and take it."

"Naim is going to London soon. You can give the meat to him, Mila Apu."

"Are you coming with him?"

"No, Mila Apu. Shrabonti's exams are starting soon. I better not."

I became very busy with home and school and a variety of other things. Sometimes I had to write articles or stories for Bangladeshi newspapers and magazines. I remember an anecdote of a German writer. Once a reader asked him, "How can you write so many big books with the other work of your everyday life? I cannot even write a letter for lack of time." "You know something?" the writer replied. "The difference between you and me is just one. I mean just one difference between a writer and a non-writer." "What is that one difference?" "After completing all our everyday work and duties, we can make time to write. Non-writers cannot do so."

I forget the name of the writer. (Thomas Mann, Günter Grass, Herta Müller?) But I remember the story when I sit at the table to write, sometimes in the middle of the night.

Busy, busy, busy! I forgot all about the holy meat and Naim's coming over to London soon. Suddenly one day the phone rang.

"Mila Apu, it's Rosie."

"What's up, Rosie? Is Naim coming over soon?"

"No, Mila Apu. His conference has been cancelled. Apu, why don't you come over for the weekend? We decorated the house so nicely, you wouldn't believe it. The spare room looks immaculate. We have a nice chair and table for you too, if you want to do bit of jotting."

"No way I can go now. Ofsted Inspectors – government appointed inspectors – are coming soon to visit our school. No time to die even. If Azrail comes I have to tell him, 'Take my soul later. At the moment I will be needing it for the Ofsteds."

"Is it that serious?"

"Yes. They will look for every reason to fail me. I have to fight back tooth and nail. It's a question of survival. If they fail me, I have a standing offer for a job, though."

"What is that?"

"To sweep the streets of London. No Ofsted there."

"Mila Apu, you are so funny." She paused a little and said, "We have to find someone who can bring the meat. Keep it in your deep fridge for the time being – if it is not too much trouble."

"No trouble at all. Shurovi is not asking for any green grass or leaves. She is sound asleep there. Inform me if you find someone to carry your holy meat."

"We will. I was wondering what portion of Shurovi was there. Is it her leg, thigh, back, neck or her heart? Could be anything."

Then I became busy doing some weekly planning for the hooligans to keep them real busy.

Two months went by. One day the phone rang again. I heard Rosie's sweet, sugary voice, "Mila Apu, Dr. Siddiq is going to London for a day. He is coming back the next day. As you know, Shrabonti's tenth birthday's on the 23rd of this month. Dr. Siddiq would not miss the birthday party for the world. So he will try to come back here by the afternoon train. Are your Ofsteds still there?"

"Just started. They will be with us for seven days – from 8 o'clock to 5 o'clock."

"Mila Apu, Dr. Siddiq will be very busy there. He will not have any time to visit you in Kent. So I tell you what would be best. Take the container of meat to your school. Dr. Siddiq will collect the meat from there. Your school will be on his way to the station."

"What a wonderful solution! Are you telling me to take Shurovi out of the freezer and bring her with me to school?"

"Would that be too difficult for you, Mila Apu?"

"They say 'difficulty' is a word in the dictionary of fools. I will manage! But you know something, Rosie? Sometimes I wonder where I can get that special edition of *Dictionary of Fools*. I need to look at it sometimes."

Rosie giggled. "You are so funny. Please do not forget to take the meat to your school."

"I will not forget."

"Thanks and sorry for all this trouble."

"No need to say 'sorry' nine hundred times, Rosie."

It was a difficult task to take out that icy container from the freezer. I had to fight with it. After a lot of pushing and pulling, the container came out, but the carrier bag in which the container had been kept was torn to bits. Never mind that! I can always make a fresh packet, I thought.

Some of the things in the freezer were screeching and squeaking in protest. I ignored them all and muttered, "Come out, Shurovi. Let's go to school."

Reenee told me Dr. Siddiq would come between 1 and 2 o'clock. My lunch break. But there was no time to have a nice lunch when the Ofsteds were inspecting and suspecting all the time. An apple was good enough at that moment. Not only Shurovi, I had to carry all my weekly, monthly and daily planning folders and some homemade games to please those toffee noses or to tell them, I'm a creative teacher. So my hands were heavy. After a lot of changing and switching buses and tubes, I reached my school at 20 past 7. I thought it would be better to keep the container in the school freezer. I had to explain everything to the school secretary, Doreen. She was not very happy at the meaty business but smiled to cheer me up. (God bless her!)

Dr. Siddiq did not come between 1 and 2, and I had to go to the third floor for the inspectors. They were not looking at my paper work through their glasses but under a microscope. They were good at scrutinising everything. But it seemed they liked my home-made games and I was feeling a bit better for it.

Old chubby Doreen climbed up all the stairs from the ground floor to the third floor to tell me that a gentleman called Dr. Siddiq was waiting for me. "You better hurry up, Miss. The gentleman said he has to catch the train shortly." Doreen was breathing heavily.

I asked permission to go to the ground floor for ten minutes. I wondered why there were no lifts and intercoms in old Victorian schools. So, like a sputnik, I climbed down to meet Dr. Siddiq and handed over the packet of holy meat to him with a sigh of relief.

"Sorry I'm late," Dr. Siddiq apologised with a nice refreshing smile.

I tried to conceal my heavy breathing, controlling it well, and ignored my lower back pain.

I handed over the packet. He gave me another smile and thanked me genuinely and was off to catch the train.

So after two months in my deep fridge, Shurovi was going to meet Rosie who loved her a lot and vice versa.

At about 9 o'clock that evening, I was going to phone Rosie to ask about the party and the meat. The phone started to ring before that.

"What a telepathy! I was going to ring you just now, Rosie. How was the party and everything? Have you got your *Qurbani* meat?"

"The party went splendidly." She paused. Her voice was not at all enthusiastic.

"What is the matter? Didn't you get the meat?"

"Dr. Siddiq had kept all his stuff overhead in the train. He brought everything down when the train reached Leeds – a three-foot doll for Shrabonti, some personal shopping, three medical books – but forgot that special packet of meat."

"What?"

"I guess it's on the train's overhead shelf or in a locker – whatever they call it."

So Shurovi was still on the train and heading for some unknown destination.

"Good luck, Shurovi, travel well," I muttered.

"Naim believes in the lost property office, Mila Apu. They are ever so good and efficient, he says!" Then she went on and on about lost property offices.

I was tired and exhausted after spending all day with those toffee noses. They were like bad dentists, trying to pull out my teeth. "Could you please tell me the colour, size and shape of the container?"Naim told me to tell you that a clear description of the container would help us to trace the packet."

I put the phone down. I had a hard day and now this news. I had to have a long, warm shower to cool my head.

Translated by Saleha Chowdhury

Proteins, Minerals, Nigella Seeds

Pola opened the front door at the first ring, thinking it might be her friend Papia. Or perhaps Otri. But she was taken by surprise when she saw the person standing there.

"You!" she exclaimed. "Why didn't you inform me you were coming?"

She paid off the taxi, picked up the suitcase, and took her mother inside.

"So . . . you didn't expect to see me!"

Her mother's tone sounded odd.

"No, I didn't mean that," Pola hastened to add. "I never thought you would leave your house and go anywhere. I've never seen you going anywhere alone."

Pola took her mother into the living room and helped her sit down. Pola lived in a tiny flat, with one mini-sized bedroom and an equally small living room. Six hundred and fifty square feet in all. A pigeon coop of a flat. She had bought it with her own earnings and savings, with no help from anyone. Next to her bedroom was a miniscule box room. Perhaps her mother could sleep there. But, would it be all right to put her there? The tiny space was tightly crammed with so many things. There was the wall *almirah* full of her books, the writing table with all her writing paraphernalia, plus the easel, brushes, paints.

An inflatable electric mattress lay folded under the bed. Kept there in case Papia or Mimi slept over. Or Otri? No, not for Otri!

"Where is your bathroom?" Pola's mother asked.

At last, when her mother emerged, fresh and beautiful, and relaxed on the bed, Pola curled up at her feet like a kitten. Pola was thirty-two and a half, her mother fifty-eight. For the last twenty years, Pola's mother had never left her own house because of one man. At least, not stayed anywhere overnight or gone sight-seeing. Pola's mother had spent the last twenty years looking after Pola's father.

For those twenty years Pola had lived in Dhaka, her mother and father in Rangpur. Pola had not visited Rangpur much in all those years though it had been her childhood home. She had lived there till she had entered college. After graduating from university, she had gone abroad for higher studies. Even after she returned, she had very rarely visited her parents in Rangpur. There had always been a distance between Pola and her father, an uneasy relationship. As a result, even when he was taken ill, Pola had not experienced any great urge to go to see him, to be at his side. However, she did visit now and then, more from a sense of duty than anything else. Still, when the news of his death reached her, she was inexplicably affected. Her body became numb and cold. She could hardly walk. With great effort she stumbled up to her bed, collapsed there, and pulled the covers over her head.

For a long while she lay there inert, buried under the covers. From time to time, her body shivered violently, the covers shook furiously. She remembered the famous pronouncement by Meursault in *The Outsider*, "The person who cannot cry at his mother's death should be hanged." She often thought that her case would be the same, that she would not be able to cry at her father's death. But she had cried. Perhaps more in regret that her relationship with her father had not been warmer, that he had been there for her when she needed a father. When she had wanted to share her childish joys and sorrows with him, when she had needed his shoulders to cry upon, he had not been there. He had always been so cold and distant that she had been too scared even to touch him. After her father dropped her to school, he would simply speed away. Pola would lift an uncertain hand to wave goodbye, only to find that he was gone. He had simply reversed the car and sped away. No sweet hug for her. These thoughts came and went as Pola lay under the covers and thought of her father. Finally, the covers grew still. It seemed as if Pola was lying under a steel plate.

Next morning, when Pola was on the phone with her mother, there was a discernable hint of emotion in her voice. Her mother, on the other end, did not break down in a flood of emotion. Was it then only a sense of duty, of responsibility, that made the daughter call? The mother and daughter had never discussed these things openly.

After a pause, Pola asked, "Should I come over, Ma?"

"How can you come now? You have just opened your boutique."

"Of course I can." Pola knew, even if she had said no, her mother would not have been overly surprised. She felt she had to go and be with her mother. Before she hung up, she asked her mother, "Ma, what were Baba's last words?"

"He died in his sleep, Pola. The night before he had struggled very hard to say something, but couldn't. That was his tragedy. He could never articulate what he wanted to say. I saw this all my life!"

Late that night, Pola called again. "How will you sleep, Ma? All by yourself! alone?"

"Why, they are all here. Besides, you are coming tomorrow, aren't you?"

Next morning Pola flew from Dhaka to Saidpur – then on to Rangpur. To spend just two days with her mother. Her father's bed was empty. A plain, white, empty bed. A distant cousin sat by the bed and recited the Quran. The fragrance of incense permeated the room. An atmosphere of purity pervaded the place. Pola's mother was wearing a plain white shari – nothing new to her. Only the sparkling diamond nose pin was missing. Pola had loved that nose pin. So then, at long last, Pola's mother had nothing but time on her hands, plenty of time. What would her mother do with so much time? Pola had curled up like a little kitten, with her head in her mother's lap, and sobbed aloud. Her mother had cried too.

Pola's mother looked so strange, so unfamiliar. A woman's body had emerged from a *burqa*, discarded after twenty long years. She looked like a woman now, a woman in all her glory. She had always been slim. Now the black and maroon shari she was wearing made her look even slimmer. She was wearing just a pair of thin gold bangles; her ears and nose were bare. That familiar chain still hung from her neck, with that familiar locket. As a child, Pola had bitten the locket so many times; it still bore the marks. Her mother unfastened the dented and tarnished chain, with the locket, and put it round Pola's neck.

"This is yours now!"

Pola knew that she would not wear the necklace. Still, to please her mother, she said, "This is mine now? How nice!"

After a little while, Pola said, "Ma, have you come to visit me? How many years has it been, Ma, since you left your house?"

Pola's mother did not reply. Instead, she stroked Pola's hair gently. "Ah, that waist-length hair. Now shorn into a bob." She sighed.

"Easier to handle."

"You did this right after going abroad?"

Pola laughed.

Pola's mother explored the tiny apartment. The bed in the bedroom was somewhat unproportionately large. She noted the print on the bedcover – of birds and elephants. Must be from her boutique, she thought. The large, cuddly teddy bear reposing on the bed made her laugh. On one wall was a picture of Pola. Next to it, a picture of them both, mother and daughter. On the wall opposite hung a painting done by Pola herself. In the cubby-hole of a box room, Pola had her easel. Her computer too. Not an inch of the space was empty. Whenever the electric mattress was inflated, the easel had to be moved.

"I will sleep here," Pola's mother declared.

"Not at all! You will sleep in my room."

"No, here. What are you painting, Pola?" She glanced at a half-finished painting.

Pola painted beautiful pictures in the time she could spare from her boutique. "Oh! That is the cover of a book. I have been commissioned to submit a total of ten. I have given a few to Otri to do. He will come this evening at six to put the finishing touches to this one. Ma, will it bother you, if he comes?"

"No, not at all. Why should it bother me?" She had heard this name, Otri, mentioned before, but had not seen him yet.

"Ma, if it is a bother, I will tell him not to come."

"Oh, no, don't do that. Ask him to come." Pola's mother stepped out onto the miniscule balcony. A few potted plants were placed here and there. Crotons and cactuses. She looked up at the sky from the ten-storey balcony, and then glanced down, at the ground below. Hastily she looked away; she suffered from a slight touch of vertigo.

Pola did not ask her mother how long she would be staying. Nor did her mother volunteer any information.

"Ma, you know Chhoto Khala lives here. Aren't you going to visit her?"

"Let me talk to her on the phone first. You know she is completely crazy." Pola's mother smiled indulgently.

Pola was struck anew by her mother's beauty, as if seeing her for the first time. Standing there on the balcony, ten storeys above the ground, they looked like two friends. Impulsively, she hugged her mother and exclaimed, "Ma, you stay right here with me. For as long as you like!"

"Pola, before he died, your father made an oral gift to you, a *heba*. You have another house, in Rangpur. In fact, there are two houses, one for you, one for me. You can take them both, if you wish."

"For the time being, Ma, both those houses are yours to take care of. My house, your house, the land, the pond, the orchards, everything."

Pola's eyes fell on the snowy patch on her mother's head. "Ma, you have to dye that patch of white hair! You still have such thick hair."

Pola's mother laughed. It felt strange to find, after twenty long years, that she could do whatever she wanted to. Whatever pleased her. Like a woman who discards her *burqa* and discovers her body for the first time! Like a woman who looks at herself again and again with wonder! Like a caterpillar which has shed its skin and emerged as a glorious butterfly! Pola stopped herself abruptly. She didn't want to think of her mother as a butterfly.

After her bath, Pola's mother came out wearing a light blue shari. Pola stared, unable to take her eyes away.

"Tomorrow we go to the hairdresser's," she declared. Her mother smiled.

Otri came that evening. Pola's mother had not met him before. She was standing on the balcony, gazing at the beauty of the sky brilliantly lit up by a myriad stars. Pola was not home. She would not be back before eight. Otri did not know about Pola's mother. Pola had completely forgotten to tell him.

Pola's mother, startled by the sound behind, turned around. She saw a male shadow.

The young man said, "Sorry."

Pola's mother wondered how the young man had got in. Then she realised that he must have a key. She had forgotten to bolt the door from inside. "You must be Otri."

"Yes, I am Otri."

Pola's mother could see Otri clearly in the light of the sitting room. She noticed that the two top buttons of his *kurta* were open, revealing his bare chest. She found herself strangely drawn to that bare spot and was unable to avert her eyes. Whether aware of her gaze or no, Otri did not hasten to fasten his buttons. She noted his broad shoulders, his thick shock of hair, and his white teeth which lit up his face when he smiled, his tanned complexion, the fancy line of his moustache.

"May I go and paint now? You see, I help Pola. It won't take me long to complete the work."

"Yes, yes, please go ahead," Pola's mother replied in a flustered voice, and hastily withdrew into her room. She remembered she had to call her younger sister, Rimi.

"Bubu, are you in Dhaka?" Rimi answered the phone on the first ring.

"Yes, yes, kiddy, it's me."

"Tell me, how are you doing?"

"Not bad."

"Have you been taking protein as I advised you? For your leg cramps?"

"Yes."

"Don't forget. Protein is your main medicine, Bubu. Oh, yes, I told you to take minerals too. Are you?"

"I had told you that I felt tired. You told me to take potassium, manganese and some other things. I do."

"In English they are called minerals, in Bangla, *khanij lobon*. Bananas, chickpeas, fruits – these contain minerals. I hope you are taking these regularly."

"I am following your advice to the letter! Are you planning to do a PhD in herbal medicine or what?"

"Our future lies in folk medicine. Did you know that there is a cure for every ailment, every disease under the sun, in trees, plants, roots, leaves, fruits. And I will prove it."

"This means you are truly contemplating a PhD."

"It's called DSc in herbal medicine, Bubu. Now, tell me, are you taking nigella seeds regularly? or *Kalojeera* in Bengali? It greatly helps with problems related to menopause – hot flushes, mood swings. I advise many people to include it in their food intake. And with good results too."

Pola's mother laughed. "As per your advice, I grind *kalojeera or nigela seed* and spread it on bread. I even brought some with me here! I have become addicted to it. I also have it with rice. Such a delicious aroma!"

"Listen, Bubu. Nowadays many women have started HRT treatment. Hormone Replacement

Therapy. But it has so many side effects. Doctors recommend HRT treatment for women after their menopause. But if you take nigella it is the same thing, because nigella is nothing but pure hormone! Remember how mother used to make `kalojeera bhorta' or smashed nigela for you after the birth of your daughter? Do you know why?"

"I remember! And I did not have to buy Ostermilk for a long time."

"That's it, Bubu! Because this nigela is nothing but pure hormone!"

"What will I do with so many hormones?"

"I suppose you enjoy mood swings, hot flushes, a burning sensation when you pass urine?"

"No! I don't . . . . But . . . ."

"No buts! Go on taking nigella, and you will never suffer hormonal imbalance."

"So . . . protein for cramps in the feet, minerals to drive away fatigue, and nigella for hormonal imbalance. Anything you say. And now that I have developed a diabetic condition, what do I do for that?"

"What do you mean by what do you do? Why, just soak some *methi* seeds in water and drink it every day. Soak it in the night, and drink the water in the morning. In English, *methi* is fenugreek. Fenugreek, fennel, and cumin belong to the same family. They keep the kidneys in good order. In English they are known as the fennel family. For the time being, just drink *methi* water."

Pola's mother burst out laughing.

Rimi scolded her from the other end. "For God's sake, Bubu, take me seriously!"

"I have been taking you seriously for the last ten years kiddy."

"I will tell you more about herbal medicine when we meet. You will live for a hundred years like the ancient ascetics. Goodness me, if only people could learn about the benefits one can get from the trees and plants that are mentioned in the *Atharvaveda*!"

"Have you read the *Atharvaveda* too?"

"Why do you think I am talking about a DSc? Spend some time with your daughter, and then come over to my place. My house is large and airy. There is a nice roof too. You will like it here. I have so many plants in my garden and on my rooftop.. Come over. I have so much to tell you."

"What are you doing now?"

"I am writing a book about the benefits of leaves of creepers and plants, of the barks of trees. Today I completed a fantastic chapter on cinnamon."

"Cinnamon? What about cinnamon?" Pola's mother was curious.

"Do you want to know? Then listen. When Vasco da Gama set out to discover the New World, he crossed the Cape of Good Hope and reached Macao. It was there that he discovered cinnamon. It is the inner bark of a tree. Its botanical name is *Cinnamum Verum*.

Its greatest benefit to both men and women is that it enhances their libido."

"Libido? What is that?"

"L-I-B-I-D-O. Sexual ability for others, for you strength to work. Like nigella!"

"Shame on you, Rimi! What are you saying?"

"The whole world is pre-occupied with this, and all you can say is, 'Shame on you'! Have you never heard the word 'viagra' mentioned?"

"Rimi, you have become too shameless."

"Wait till the book comes out and you will soon find out how little of 'shamelessness' you have seen up to now." Then, after a slight pause, Rimi added, "Bubu, I know these things departed from your life ages ago. Sorry, Bubu, for mentioning all these."

"Go on. You don't have to say 'sorry' now!"

"Do you know what happened after cinnamon was discovered? Trouble began to brew between the Portuguese and the Dutch. The price of cinnamon started to spiral. For by then people had come to know about the benefits of this spice. Do you actually think Vasco da Gama set out on his voyage only to discover new lands? Of course not! It was first and foremost a quest for these valuable spices. Arab scientists had started researching its special qualities. Do you know, in those days women would rub cinnamon powder on their hair. And, at night, they would keep a piece of it in their mouths! You can also keep a piece of cinnamon in your mouth. It will reduce sugar in your urine. Do you know why these women chewed cinnamon and kept it in their mouths at night?"

"You don't have to tell me. I know! LIBIDO!"

"Good! You're getting there." She laughed and added, "I have so much to tell you! When are you coming?"

More of such conversation followed. At last the sisters hung up.

"She is still the same," Pola's mother thought, highly amused. She loved her younger sister, who was sixteen years younger than her.

"I am leaving now." Otri's voice broke into her reverie. His work was over for the day. It had been hot; he had opened another button, exposing more of his chest. The fan had ruffled his hair. As Pola's mother stood by him, a heady smell of deodorant mingled with perspiration accosted her. She began to blush furiously. "I will return tomorrow to finish the work. At around six in the evening. Will you be home?"

Otri had recognised her as Pola's mother. He had seen the picture of mother and daughter hanging on the wall.

"Pola won't be home. She returns at eight. I will be here, though."

Otri laughed and said, "I know."

As he passed by Pola's mother, his body brushed against her lightly.

Hastily, Pola's mother shut the door.

Another face, from long ago, of another youth, flawless and beautiful, floated up, unbidden, to her mind. That body, moist with perspiration, emanating a strong smell of cologne, that beautiful body!

Rimi's words played ping pong in her mind. What horrid words she had uttered: "Libido. Nigella seeds. Hormones. Cinnamon. Viagra." What rubbish Rimi talked. She had always been like that. She wiped her face with the end of her shari.

Pola returned at night. "Remember, Ma, tomorrow you dye your hair. And, yes, also get a trim."

"I understand colouring. But why the trim?"

"You will understand why after it is done!"

Pola's mother pondered something for a while, and then, abruptly, she asked, "Are you marrying Otri?"

"I may. Haven't decided yet."

"You have known each other for four years. Still can't decide?"

"Ma, you knew Baba for thirty-five years. Do you think you have understood him?"

Pola's mother did not answer. After a while Pola changed the topic. "Ma, you can be called *kakbondha* – isn't that the word? The mother of a single child. I am your only child."

"Not really. I did have a boy after you. I lost him in the seventh month. After that nothing but guilt and blame."

"It would have been such fun to have a little brother!"

Pola's mother sighed. "I longed for a son too. But it did not happen. I had nothing to give your father, nothing, except for my devotion and care. I spent my entire life looking after him. But your father was unable to reciprocate my devotion. Not everyone has the ability to accept the devotion of others, you know."

Mother and daughter remained silent for a while. Then Pola's mother said, "If you don't want to marry Otri, choose someone else. After all, you are above thirty already."

"Ma, is it necessary to get married?"

"The alternative, you know, is a lonely life."

"Am I lonely, Ma? With so many friends around me?"

Pola's mother had not seen her daughter from so close, for many years. They had developed in different ways; there was a vast difference in their ways of thinking, in their sense of values. The two years in Sweden had changed Pola.

"A lot of friends don't replace everything. Don't you want children? You just said it would have been nice to have had a little brother."

"That can happen anytime. Is it necessary to marry for that?"

Pola's mother stared at her daughter in utter shock. "What do you mean, Pola?" She switched on the powerful light. "What do you mean, Pola? Living together? Single parent family, like in the West?

Those don't work in our society, you know very well!"

Pola laughed and hugged her mother.

"Ah – got scared, didn't you? Don't worry about me, Ma. And tomorrow your hair, then a facial."

"Why?"

"Because I say so! You will feel relaxed. The girls will pamper you. Massage your hair, your face. You will hear music. You'll see, it will make you feel good. Then, when you see yourself in the mirror, you will not recognise yourself. You will have been transformed!"

"Oh, all right. I see, I will have to beautify myself for your sake."

When Otri came at six that evening, he could not recognise Pola's mother at first. Shining raven-black hair, smartly cut and styled, crowned her head. Her face glowed radiantly.The fringe on her forehead, cut under the expert supervision of the hairdresser, transformed her appearance. Her lips were painted a soft *maloti*-blossom pink.

Pola's mother understood that Otri was not only surprised, but also fascinated. Otri came up close to her. They started to talk. Did he want to tell her, "It feels nice to stand close to you?" Ma laughed as she stood chatting with him, completely engrossed. Today she could smell a different cologne on him. It had been ages since she had laughed like this.

Otri's glance fell on her freshly painted nails, her well-groomed arms and feet, the cheerful expression on her face. "How beautiful she would look on canvas," Otri thought. He would call that painting "Woman." The soft scent of her attar wafted up to him. She looked fetching in her fuchsia shari and her red blouse with a floral pattern embroidered on the sleeves. Red gemstone earrings adorned her ears, small but becoming. Otri had seen these earrings on Pola. Pola's mother had picked them up from Pola's dressing table and put them on.

A bright half moon shone in the star-studded sky. A gentle breeze blew in the balcony, lifting the *anchal* of her shari and causing it to gently brush against Otri.

The tiny balcony seemed to have fulfilled its purpose with them standing there. In the midst of her conversation, Pola's mother glanced at the ground below and suddenly felt dizzy. It was the old vertigo. She lost her balance, was on the verge of falling. Otri swiftly stretched out his arms and caught her just in time. He held her tightly in his strong arms. She seemed to have difficulty breathing. Slowly, recovering her balance, she disengaged herself from Othri's arms, hot and feverish all over.

"Would you like to go to your room? To rest?"

Pola's mother nodded, all confused and embarrassed. She went into the bedroom and collapsed on the bed, clutching the teddy bear in a tight embrace. Light and shadow played havoc around her. Otri came to the the door of her room to say something, perhaps to ask if she wanted some water. Then he changed his mind. He emerged from the darkness into the light, lost in his thoughts.

He did not work that evening. Swiftly he descended the stairs, stepped out into the real world, his feet on the solid earth.

"Ma, how could you just leave without even telling me?" Pola scolded her mother over the phone, several days later.

"I wasn't feeling too well. And I suddenly remembered an unfinished task. Something important I had to take care of."

"You didn't go to Chhoto Khala's house, either."

"She is so busy with her book on herbal medicine. I didn't want to disturb her."

After that there was a brief silence on the other end. Was there something Pola wanted to say? Then she asked, "Ma are you going on Hajj this year?"

"No. Why do you ask?"

Pola didn't answer. After a while she said, "Ma, I will visit you soon, spend some time with you. After a short stay with you, I want to take you to Darjeeling. Just you and me. You have not been anywhere for a long time. Did you know, now-a-days one can go to Darjeeling by bus? Up to Siliguri, and by jeep from there. We will go for seven days. We will see the sunrise. We will really enjoy ourselves. Your legs are okay still. No joint pains, arthritis. Do you follow Chhoto Khala's advice?"

"Just you and me?" Pola's mother could not understand what her daughter meant.

"Just you and me! Again those four words! "Ma, do you remember those stories?"

"The ones I used to tell you? To put you to sleep?"

"Yes, those. Ma, you left your jars of nigella and minerals here. I will bring them when I come."

"No, no. You don't have to bother. One does not need all those to keep one's body fit."

"Oh, you don't want to keep fit then!"

"I will be fine without those. Your Chhoto Khala wants me to be her guinea pig. She is completely crazy!"

When they finished talking, it was late at night. Pola's mother went into her kitchen. She remembered the unfamiliar face in the mirror. The face and body that had shed twenty years. "Did I go into the bedroom that night because of vertigo?" She did not know the real reason. Her mind was in turmoil. Why had she lain on that bed with sleek satin sheets, tightly clutching the teddy bear? Her body moist with perspiration as the footsteps sounded from outside the door?

Nigella seeds, cinnamon, hormones, libido – she flung them all out from her window. They flew out like winged birds in flight! All those nigella seeds, bay leaves, cinnamon, cardamom, cloves. All! Who knows what elements they contained? That night had been a half-moon night; tonight the moon was full. A lunatic night!

Translated by Shahruk Rahman

The Disappearance of Gopal Maker

At Hili, on one side of the rail track is Pakistan and on the other, India. Gopal Maker was a bicycle mechanic. When Pakistan was born, all of Gopal Maker's relations migrated to the Indian side. His maternal uncle, maternal aunt, his elder brother and his brother's children. Even his wife, Komola, left. Only he didn't go.

He said, "This is my country. How can I leave my own home?"

Dangling her nose ring, his wife snapped at him, "If you get killed, what good will your country be?"

"You go ahead! Don't worry about me." They didn't have any children, his wife was infertile.

Leaving with her belongings, accompanied by all their relations, his wife turned back to him. Covering her eyes with her *anchal*, she cried, "You don't want to go today, but you'll be forced to leave tomorrow when the Muslims make your life miserable."

"Wait for me. See when I come."

The parrot hanging in a cage in the empty one-room hut was delighted that there was at least one person left behind to feed him.

"Happy? It's just you and me. You will look after me and I will look after you."

Wagging its tail, the bird called out, "Gopal, Gopal."

Gopal watered the basil bush in the courtyard. Lying on his lonesome bed, he watched the posts of his hut absent-mindedly. Then, suddenly, he shook off his lethargy.

He was about thirty. His real surname was Barui but he was better known as Gopal Maker. He sat down in his cycle repair shop and began working as he usually did. Immaculate work.

A few persons asked him, "Gopal, why didn't you go?"

"This country is mine. She is my mother. How can I leave my own mother?"

Some were happy and some weren't at what he said. Those who wanted to take possession of his business were disappointed.

Panchu Katani said, "But you're a Hindu. Go to a Hindu state. Why do you want to stay here?"

Gopal Maker didn't respond. He carried on with his work quietly.

The matter didn't end there. A number of people began frequently commenting about his caste and creed. Those who wanted to get hold of his business and his spick-and-span one-roomed hut were enraged. Gopal Maker ignored them.

Although he ignored what people were saying, he realised that the issue of religion had now grown to be a big problem. With the new Pakistani zeal, verbal abuse pelted on him like stones from everywhere. However, even when his shop was set on fire one day, he was still determined not to leave.

After repairing his shop, he went straight to the mosque to meet Moulana Hakimpuri.

The moulana knew him well. He was taken aback to see him, "*Malauns* are not allowed to enter mosques."

Gopal Maker bent down and touched the moulana's feet, "Moulana Hakimpuri, please make me a musolman."

The moulana was a little surprised. Converting a non-believer meant his seven generations would find a place in heaven! Their visas to heaven would be confirmed. Why should he let go this great opportunity? He converted Gopal to Islam before a number of witnesses. He made him recite the *kalma*, the declaration of faith in Allah and His Prophet. He distributed *batasha*, sugar candies light as air. He made him drink water from the holy Zamzam spring. A doctor's compounder made him more of a Muslim with a surgical knife, under his lungi. Then he was a complete Muslim. In addition to this he was given a new name – Mohammed Gopal Maker. A few persons started calling him Mohammed but his real name, Gopal, remained stuck to his body like skin. A prayer mat, a *tasbih* for reciting the holy words, and a *bodna* to perform his ablution before prayers were sent to him. Hakimpuri gave him a Bangla translation of the

Quran. "It isn't enough that you converted to Islam. You need to understand this religion properly as well."

Those who had set fire to his shop were definitely defeated. They cursed him, "*Shala*! How are we to beat a *malaun's* intelligence? Let's chalk out another plan. How can we possess both his cycle repair shop and his house?" He's turned into the apple of Moulana Hakimpuri's eye!"

Gopal Maker came to say his prayers with a white cap on his head. When Hakimpuri led the prayers in scorching heat, Gopal would hold an umbrella above his head. He stood motionless behind Hakimpuri during the *khutba*, the sermon before Friday prayers. He never failed to hold the umbrella for Hakimpuri on large congregations such as Eid. Hakimpuri also enjoyed his services.

One midnight, Gopal quietly brought out a Shiva linga from underneath his bed and prayed, "Shiva Thakur, please don't be mad at me. I am a Muslim in name only. I had to become a Muslim to stay here. You're everything to me. I cannot leave my country and ancestral home and live anywhere else. My umbilical cord was buried here after I was born. This is my own land, Shiva Thakur."

No one saw him praying to Shiva. Who could see what Gopal was doing in the middle of the night? The other gods and goddesses also quietly had their share of worship and flower offerings. Gopal's ancestral faith remained hidden underneath his bed. The rest of the time he was a Muslim.

This was how Gopal survived the Hindu-Muslim conflict. He heard from people that his wife had fallen in love with a shopkeeper and had moved to Balurghat with him. Komola said, "The man who has renounced his ancestral religion cannot be my husband anymore. How could he? He must have been possessed. I know there was a *petni,* a female demon, on top of the tamarind tree next to our house. She must have done this."

Gopal heard all this but it didn't make any difference to him. Nonetheless, he stood before the cage of Khushi the parrot and said in a slightly choking voice, "They've all gone. I have closed the doors to that country myself. Please don't leave me, Khushi." Khushi wiggled her tail in assurance.

"Gopal, get married again. Fatema is not that old. She has already lost two husbands. Marry her and give her shelter."

"Let her do my chores. I can't marry her."

Fatema came to his house to do his chores. She swept the courtyard but she could not clean the interior of his house.

Gopal warned her, "Fatema, don't you ever go inside my room." His personal treasures – the Shiva linga, Lakshmi and Durga's icons – were all hidden underneath his bed. Those were his alone.

"Why, what riches of seven kings have you hidden in your room that I can't enter? Let me sweep your room. It needs to be cleaned. You keep your room so untidy! Clothes hanging on ropes and the floor not swept and wiped! Without a woman's touch can a house be organised, foolish Gopal?"

"No, you don't! Let me be. Do the other stuff. You don't have to worry about my house."

"What other work? Sweeping the veranda, collecting dry leaves from the courtyard as fuel – this is all the work I have. You don't even eat meat. Just a little vegetable and fish curry. How much time does that take? A fine cow has been slaughtered today. Why don't I fetch some meat and cook it for you?"

"No. I don't eat meat."

"You're a Muslim only in name. You're still a Hindu at heart."

"Why? One can't be a Muslim if one doesn't eat meat?"

"Of course one can. But you haven't really converted, that is for sure."

"Don't talk so much. Water the flower plants and clean the cage of the parrot. Wash a few clothes. Sweep and wipe the place."

"Why aren't you cutting down the basil?"

"It's good for curing colds. I will one day. What are you trying to say?"

"Marry me. Then you won't have to pay me for my chores. Just provide me food and clothes, and I will be your wife. Wives have dignity. What dignity do maids have?"

"No, I can't marry you. Why are you saying this? Have I disrespected you somehow?"

"Why not? Why can't you marry me? Don't you have a young man's blood flowing in your vain, Gopal?" Fatema smiled in amusement. "Sleep with me one day. You'll be surprised to know how wonderful I can be!"

"Just get lost. Never mention all this again."

"Why not? I see, you probably have some problem. I can fix your problem. I've given pleasure to two husbands. One of them had an accident on the rail track and the other died falling off a date tree while collecting date juice."

"That's why. I might die in some mishap if I marry you."

"Can't people sleep together without marriage?"

"Now get lost. Don't bother me again."

"I see. You can't forget Komola. She's never going to return. She eloped with a shopkeeper. They live in Balurghat now as husband and wife."

"Don't ever repeat this again."

But Fatema did not let go so easily. Although she could never enter Gopal's room, she longed for a chance to do so.

"Gopal, what's the matter? Why do you always hold the umbrella over my head? No one does that for me."

Moulana Hakimpuri asked him one day after his prayers.

Gopal did not respond. Just sat there, his head bent.

"Rain or sun. Every time I stand up to give a speech or the *khutba*, I notice you holding the umbrella above me for hours."

They were sitting quietly under a tree. There was no one near them.

"I have to pray on the terrace. When the mosque expands, I won't have to pray there anymore. You do the same at the Eid congregation. Tell me the truth. Why do you do this?"

"Huzoor, can I speak to you frankly?"

Moulana Hakimpuri smiled. "Of course. Speak frankly. Say whatever you have stored inside. No one's here."

"Huzoor, I was Hindu for the last thirty-five years. You believe God is one. We need to fear Him. However, Hindus find their gods even in human beings. For example, a guest is our god. You speak of such beautiful things for so long. While listening to you, I can't help thinking you are my Allah, my Bhagwan."

"*Tauba, tauba.* Blasphemy! What are you saying? I, Allah? I am a sinner, a sinful human being, Gopal."

"I do not know all that. You say not to worship anyone but Allah. But all I can say is I can spend the rest of my life under your feet."

"Hindus worship even cows. Would you still consider doing this after so many years of being a Muslim?"

"I will not say that, Huzoor. What I will say is how can we kill the mother who gives us milk? Huzoor, how can one kill the mother cow which has given us milk since childhood?"

"Have you read *Sura Bakara*? I gave you the Quran in Bangla. Did you read it? As soon as the prophet Moses left, the Israelites made a golden calf and began worshipping it. They had forgotten God. Do you think they did the right thing?"

"I don't think so. But how can we slaughter a cow that gives us milk, Huzoor?" He said the same again.

Moulana Hakimpuri smiled slightly. He only chided the man who considered him a god and held the umbrella over his head for hours. "You need to understand the whole concept of Islam. You haven't yet completely become a Muslim. Don't talk about this with others. You'll be in trouble if you do. You also worship rocks!"

"But, Huzoor, through worshipping it, the rock one day turns into god. It's all about devotion, Huzoor. Everything is possible through true devotion."

"I will always remain Moulana Hakimpuri. I will never turn into your god, remember that. No matter how much you worship me, I am just a sinful human being."

"Whatever you say, my devotion for you will never cease. Whenever I see you suffering in the sun or rain, I will hold the umbrella for you. If you feel hot, I will fan you. You are a sufi. You help others." Gopal took off his shirt and began fanning Moulana Hakimpuri with it.

"That's enough. You don't have to display your devotion any more. Go, read the Quran carefully tonight. See what is written in it. I will take your test in seven days. Are you praying regularly?"

"Yes, Huzoor."

"What do you pray for?"

"I pray for everyone's well-being."

Hakimpuri smiled. "Read the Holy Quran. It is worthy of everyone's faith and devotion. That is why it is so powerful."

"I will, Huzoor."

Gopal Maker held the umbrella above Moulana Hakimpuri's head and reached him home. Wherever there was a muddy patch, he placed bricks for him to step on.

In the evening, he returned home after doing his own work. He was taken aback. Fatema was standing in the moonlit courtyard like the majestic moon. She was wearing a red shari revealing the curves of her body. She had adorned her forehead with a red *teep*. She had bangles on her wrists and a garland round her neck. Her lips were red with *alta*.

Gopal Maker spoke curtly, "What are you doing here? Go home."

"I'm not going home. Today you will take me into your room. You will let me sit on your bed. And then . . . ."

"Again you're saying the same things. Didn't I tell you not to say all this again?"

"Why not? Am I ugly? Don't you have a man's blood flowing in your veins?"

Gopal Maker chased her off and locked his gate. "Go where your tricks will work."

"I am not a whore, you know. I love you, Gopal. Why don't you understand?"

"Fine. Tell me this tomorrow in broad daylight. Not in the darkness of night. Now go. I won't let you in if you ever repeat these things."

Fatema hissed like an angry cobra. "It is not good to be so proud. See what I do to you. You will keep on humiliating me like this every day and I will continue to tolerate it? That will not be."

Fatema had decided what she would do. She would break the lock of his room and see what he had hidden there. Had he hidden another woman in his room?

"O Shiva Thakur, O Ma Lakshmi, O Ma Kali, I have been neglecting you. I hope you are all right." He sat down to do puja. He had also prayed earlier, "Dear Allah of the Muslims and Bhagwan of the Hindus, please bestow your blessings upon all human beings."

He also planned to read the entire Quran. Moulana Hakimpuri was a good man. He would not lie to him.

The parrot seemed to be in a listless state. Maybe it had grown old. It was not eating anything. Gopal stroked the bird affectionately.

The next evening when he returned home, he received a shock. His idols of Shiva, Lakshmi, Kali, Ganesh, Kartik were all rolling about in the courtyard. The parrot was dead in its cage.

Fatema came first. A host of others came after her.

"*Shala, malaun!* You bastard Hindu! You kept these idols in the same room where you kept the Holy Quran, the *tasbih,* and the picture of the Ka'aba. Tomorrow we will tell Moulana Hakimpuri everything. Then we will pour whey on your head and send you to the other side of the border. Have you become a Muslim? Can you become a true Muslim just by snipping that piece of flesh? How dare you?"

Fatema smiled in amusement. "Today is Gopal Maker's last day. I will see what punishment you receive before I go. You would not let me into your room and this is what you did. Shameful, disgusting!"

"*Shala*, bastard, you worship the Shiva linga? See if we do not cut off yours tomorrow!"

Gopal Maker remained silent and said nothing.

The next morning the sky was overcast. Moulana Hakimpuri told the villagers to thrust Gopal Maker across the border, but not to kill him.

"What are you saying, Huzoor? We should crush his bones."

Moulana Hakimpuri said again, "Just do what I said. Give him one push through the barbed wire fence – the way sugar, rice, clothes, sharis, and spices are smuggled. Not through the legal path of the BDR."

Black clouds covered the sky. It would start to pour any moment. A number of *lathiyal*, skilled stick fighters, surrounded his house. They yelled at Gopal to come out if he wanted to save his life. But no one emerged from the house. The door was open. The door had been locked from the outside. Who the hell had unlocked the door? The people next door had been awake the whole night; even they were unaware of what had happened. Gopal Maker had taken nothing with him. One of them had scissors to cut off his hair and another had a pot of whey to carry out his punishment publicly. Everyone agreed he couldn't be sent across the border this easily! "*Shala*, is he anybody's son-in-law that he can be sent all clean and well-dressed?"

Gopal was nowhere to be seen. He had been so terrified that he must have fled the previous night. But no one could tell which way Gopal had gone. The people who spent the whole night at the border smuggling sharis, clothes, sugar, and rice had not seen him. None of the border guards had seen him anywhere.

"*Shala*, which way did he escape then?"

174

Finally, everyone left in frustration. They helped themselves to his possessions and left, cursing him.

When the racket had quietened down, Moulana Hakimpuri came and stood in front of the house. The basil podium was still there. Fatema had said that he wouldn't let the basil be cut because it could cure colds. It was a neat house.

The water in the well was ice-cold. So many people had quenched their thirst here. The cool water of this well was unparalleled. Even the smugglers, who smuggled sugar and rice across the border, had quenched their thirst with its cool water every time they passed by. Gopal would tell them, "You will be punished one day for your sins. He is watching us from above. You're thirsty now. Leave after quenching your thirst."

He had not flung himself into the well either. The well had been checked. Where did this whole person disappear?

Moulana Hakimpuri kept standing there. The sky was overcast with black clouds. What was Moulana Hakimpuri trying to see, rubbing his eyes?

Where was Gopal going through the clouds with an umbrella over his head? To meet that Someone who was believed to live up there, but had never come down to earth and shown human beings the exact way to reach Him? Human beings had prescribed different ways according to their own whims. And because of these different paths, there had been so much conflict, so much bloodshed. At times, rivers of blood had flowed through the land.

Moulana Hakimpuri glanced up. Mohammad Gopal Maker was not there anymore. Neither was Gopal's umbrella. Only clouds.

Translated by Masrufa Ayesha Nusrat

Moses

It was midnight. Clutching her chest, Miriam collapsed on the bed. She had suffered a massive heart attack. A few years ago she had a mild one. She gasped for breath like a fish out of water. Her eyes rolled upwards.

Isaac Perring got up from the bed next to her and came up to her. He had just fallen asleep after a hard day going over his accounts. He switched the light on and asked in a sleepy voice, "What is wrong, Miriam?"

Miriam's pet, the beautiful Bathsheba, was perched in her cage nearby. She had been flapping her wings desperately a little while ago, probably trying to let everyone know that Miriam was in trouble. Now she sat quietly, looking around now and then. The nine-year-old cat, Moses, appeared and walked around before walking away. The highland terrier, Ruth, sat by the door. She shook her white, majestic fur as she got up to look around. She then put her head on her paws and went back to sleep.

"What has happened, Miriam?" Isaac asked.

Miriam lay quiet, save for a strange gurgling sound in her throat. She had stopped gasping for breath. She was lying inert, as if she had again fallen asleep after a nightmare. He could have picked up the phone to call a doctor. But he gave up the idea of doing so. He would call the doctor in the morning. Even though their homes in Tel Aviv were in the same neighbourhood, he knew that he would have to pay the doctor if he visited her at night. The doctor usually took only a couple of pounds from people from his own country, but, if he came at this hour of the night, he would charge him ten pounds at the least. So Isaac Perring refrained from calling the doctor.

It wasn't unusual for Miriam to have a gurgling noise in her throat. It wasn't unusual either for her to wake up from a nightmare. He couldn't imagine that his wife, his companion of forty years, had already torn off all her bindings to this earth and left for good. He was seventy-five and he didn't know anything apart from his shop and his business.

Being incarcerated in a Nazi concentration camp as a child, he had been almost brainwashed. For him all food and drink were precious. He remembered how his heart had beaten faster when he had found a piece of white bread. He and his parents had miraculously escaped from the camp, and white bread had rained like manna from the sky. Was there anything more beautiful in the whole world than that piece of white bread? Isaac didn't think it was possible. The whole village had been elated when bread had rained from the heavens above. But their joy could not compare with Isaac's joy. Why? Because those villagers didn't know about the atrocities that had been carried out in the concentration camp; they didn't know how humanity had failed. They hadn't screamed in pain; they hadn't heard those who screamed in pain.

If he looked around, he might be able to find a bottle of barley water. But, exhausted with the work of going over his business accounts, Isaac didn't look for it. He was very tired and went to sleep. So Miriam died without having even a drop of water that night. And Isaac couldn't perform his last duty to his wife. Well, not quite the last, it would have been his second-last duty. He had a tough time while performing his last duty: all his calculations regarding the funeral were proved wrong.

In the morning, when the first rays of light fell on Miriam's face, Isaac realised that his petite, quiet wife would never talk again. That she wouldn't follow him around all over the house like a shadow anymore.

No one knew if it was because of the torture of the Germans that Isaac had fathered no children even though he and Miriam were married for forty years. Miriam acquired a dog, a cat, and a bird as pets and showered them with her maternal love. Undoubtedly they were sad at losing their mother. The beautiful Bathsheba didn't spread her wings anymore. Moses roamed around the house with a long face. Ruth too brooded in her own way for a long time. Finally, the doctor had to be called. He declared Miriam dead and wrote the death certificate. But he didn't take any fees as he was from Israel.

After taking care of all the formalities, Isaac Perring realised that he would have to spend a lot of money for the three animals, absolutely unnecessary pennies and pounds. Miriam used to earn twenty pounds per week as she helped Isaac in the shop. She had started with five pounds per week, which had increased to ten and then, for the next ten years, had been twenty. Miriam had not had any increment in the past ten years. But she had never complained. She used to spend ten to twelve pounds on her pets. She was happy to do so. For her it was neither a burden nor did she think of it as a waste. The question never arose. What other pastime did she have other than working in the shop, helping her husband, cooking and tidying the house? She saved her extra pounds and pennies in a large powder box. When she died, Isaac pounced on the box. He murmured, "Gosh! Funerals are so expensive!"

Even if everything was done very simply, one needed at least a white Rolls Royce hearse and lots of flowers. One had to pay for the grave too. There might have been some discounts offered for funeral services, but Isaac must have missed seeing them because of his busy schedule. That is why Miriam's funeral proved quite expensive. It's a mystery why he didn't cremate her.

Everything was soon over. For a few months, he postponed the thought of hiring someone to help. He wanted to make up for the money he had lost at the funeral. He must have thought, "Let me manage as long as I can!" The person who came in twice a week to stock the shelves had to be paid quite a bit. How could he afford to hire another person? And this person wouldn't be like Miriam, who worked day and night for only twenty pounds. Anyone else would charge at least fifty pounds! No, he would see about it later. He thought to himself how well Miriam had worked with that four-foot-eleven-inch stature of hers. No one else would ever get up on a stepladder and say, "Couldn't you make me a bit taller, Lord? Anything I do, I need to get on a ladder!"

This thought would have depressed him if Miriam had not left the three pets behind. Their breakfast, lunch, and dinner – the cans and cardboard boxes of Whiskas, GoCat, Dana, Pal – didn't walk home. They had to be bought from stores. He had to spend quite a bit of money. As he bought them, Isaac Perring felt quite irritated with his wife. He would grumble, "Why didn't you take them along with you when you left?" Moses got several kicks from Issac. His crime was that he walked around Isaac's feet, trying to tell him that he was hungry. Ruth was beaten with a stick for barking "Give me something to eat! Give me something to eat!" Isaac hung Bathsheba's cage so low that Moses managed to separate the bird's feathers from her body. He had finally proven his manhood. Bathsheba's feathers fluttered all over the balcony.

Miriam had first seen Bathsheba in a pet shop. She was dark bottle green in colour and was wearing a bright red dress. She had a red scarf around her neck. She even had red lipstick on. She looked like a fairy. She was sitting quietly in her cage. Miriam had gone to buy food for Ruth and Moses. She came back home with their food in one hand and a cage in the other. She had got Moses earlier from the same shop, when he was just ten days old. He looked like a cotton ball. He seemed to have kohl lining his eyes. His body was soft and tender. She would hold him in the palm of her hand and feed him milk with a dropper. Now he was huge. When he stretched out his body and slept, he covered Miriam's entire bed.

Bathsheba's red and green feathers were all over the balcony. But Isaac was relieved. There was one less mouth to feed. "There are two more to feed," he said aloud. They also needed to eat as long as they were alive. All night he wondered how he could get rid of them. Finally, in the morning, he came up with a plan.

He told the shelf filler, "Work on your own. I am just coming back." Isaac knew she wouldn't be able to steal anything, for his brain was like a computer. He knew exactly where he had put what. In fact, even when he was asleep, he could locate what was on which shelf. He would know in seconds if there was something missing. The girl knew that too. He just told her, "Don't leave the shop till I come!"

The human computer with his cyclopedic brain went to Bartashi Dog Home. Sitting in the back of the pickup, Ruth must have thought that she was going on an outing. She barked in joy. Miriam used to put a chain round Ruth's neck and take her for walks between her chores. Ruth had never been anywhere else. What a boring life!

The huge dog keeper put a big collar on Ruth's neck and told Isaac, "Thank you for bringing the stray dog. I will keep her here."

Isaac returned home in happy spirits. So now he was left with only Moses. The girl was still working. She would clean up the shop after filling the shelves. She got fifteen pounds working two days a weeks. He remembered that Miriam took five pounds more. But if he had considered this with a cool brain, he would have realised that Miriam worked from seven in the morning to seven in the evening and would have known that she didn't charge too much. He felt dizzy whenever he thought of money. His computerised brain didn't have any place for emotions.

For a month Isaac Perring didn't have to worry about Moses' food since his wife had stocked seven cans of Whiskas and two cans of GoCat in the larder. Giving the cat the last of his ten red biscuits, he said, "After this, you will get just water. Nothing else!"

Moses answered with a purr and watched him. He was not the prophet Moses, so he felt hungry and thirsty just like an ordinary creature. Alas, who would call him lovingly? Between her daily chores or after completing her work, who would shake a cardboard box and call, "Mose! Mose! Come and eat"? And, after he began eating, who would caress his back and say, "Finish your food and go to sleep! Don't disturb me while I am at work. Okay?" Moses would meow in affirmation.

Where had those days gone?

Moses lost his fluffiness. He looked scruffy and scrawny. Who was going to give him a bath once a week and dry his fur with a drier? No one cared if he didn't look clean anymore.

Every night, when he came to sleep, Isaac found Moses fast asleep on the bed, smelling of his dead wife. Isaac felt like throwing Moses out of the window. He would surely fall under some bus or lorry and then he could go and live with Miriam in heaven. No, he would leave that for now. It wasn't a very difficult task. It would take only minutes. All he had to do was lift the window screen and throw him out.

Moses made the same rumbling noises that Miriam used to when he slept. Each time he walked around Isaac's feet, he would get a violent kick. He would then go and sit on the wall, or escape into the garden. He would return only when it was time to sleep. Isaac smiled like a disciple of the Marquis De Sade when he saw the famished Moses. Sometimes he saw Moses as Hess or Goebbels or Mengele. When Moses cried out of hunger, Isaac was reminded of his childhood when he had gone hungry for many days. He thought to himself, "Now see what it feels like when you don't get anything to eat." He remembered how he had once got a hot charcoal on his palm instead of food.

Then he hummed the song "Shalom, Shalom" to himself.

One evening when he had finished his work, he saw someone at the door. He had been engrossed in counting the day's money by the dim light of the lamp. His eyesight was still good so he had no problem working in a low light. He only had soup and white bread. Who knows how he kept well the whole year on that diet?

Hearing the knock, he asked, "Who is it?"

A deep voice answered, "It's me. Rabbi Nicholas."

Isaac quickly opened the door to let the rabbi in. He couldn't live in the Jewish community without respecting the head of their religious community. Even though he couldn't make time to go the synagogue regularly because of work, he celebrated Yom Kippur and Rosh Hashanah and observed the Sabbath. The rabbi walked in with a serious countenance and the yashmulke which he always wore.

"Shalom."

"Shalom." He asked Isaac how he had been. Finally, he came to the purpose of his visit. He was planning to open an old home for the elderly people of the Jewish community. He wanted a donation.

Isaac's face grew pale at the word "donation." His throat went dry and he felt dizzy. He had occasionally given a donation to the rabbi, but he understood that this time the donation would not be just ten or twelve pounds. It would be much more. It would be easier to give the rabbi one of his ribs than money. Isaac didn't have many needs. He was alone so he could donate about twenty thousand pounds. Couldn't he? This was dangerous math. His mental data sheet was torn to bits.

He asked in a dry voice, "Would you like some tea?"

He thought that the rabbi would say, "No thanks," the way everyone else does. "No need to bother." But the rabbi didn't say what people usually do.

So Isaac put on the electric kettle and made two mugs of tea. He found some stale biscuits in the can. Biscuits took time in Britain to become stale due to lack of humidity. His biscuits didn't look too bad. In fact, they looked like ten gold coins inside the jar.

The rabbi had tea and biscuits. Then he changed the topic. "Why don't you remarry, Isaac? You are not that old! There is not another hard-working person like you in our community. You are quiet and amiable, and that's why I admire you."

Isaac listened to the rabbi while he stirred his tea. Everybody liked the rabbi; he was a friend of the community.

The rabbi had long wished to build an old home for the Jewish community. He believed that once he had built the structure, people would donate freely. It was the beginning that was hard.

After finishing the stale biscuits, he dangled a bait in front of Isaac. "I have a relation, a widow. She is childless. She would be around forty or forty-two. But she looks twenty-five. She will remarry only if she finds someone good. If she found someone like you, Isaac, she would be very happy!"

Isaac was not at all happy with this proposal. If a woman of forty looked twenty-five, she would definitely wear a lot of makeup, uses masses of cosmetics, and be on vitamin pills. He also knew that he would never get anyone who would be as easily pleased as Miriam used to be. He couldn't help but think of Miriam at that moment. Not so much of Miriam, but of how little she needed to keep her happy.

The rabbi had finished talking. It was getting late. He suddenly mentioned the amount he needed.

Isaac felt as if someone had pierced his heart with nine million needles. He turned blue and said in a dry voice, "Where would I get so much money? I don't have that kind of money."

"How much can you donate then?"

The rabbi was very clever. When people wish to climb to the top of a tree, they must at least reach the branches. But he was still not sure if he could reach the branch, or whether he would have to rub his horns against its trunk, or perhaps even sit at the root of the tree for eternity! Isaac was not willing to commit any amount. But the rabbi only got up when Isaac promised that he would donate some money.

"Shalom, Isaac. I will be back in two days. I will be busy tomorrow. The day after, a rabbi from Bradford is supposed to come to meet me. So I will come the day after that. Is that okay?"

He turned around at the door. "I am going to Israel in a few days. I will stay in a kibbutz for about a month. I have an architect brother. I also have a cousin who is a civil engineer. I will discuss the blueprint of the old home with them. You see I am very serious about it. All I need now is your help."

There was no problem with the rabbi's saying all those things while leaving. It was the mention of money that ruined everything. Isaac felt as though nine million needles were piercing his heart.

After finishing his work, Isaac entered his house. The shop was in front; the house at the rear. The house was poorly lit. Isaac intentionally maintained an impoverished façade. He had bought the house from a friend quite a long time ago. He had paid almost nothing for it. He had turned the large drawing room into the shop. He sold many different things in the shop. It was a mini market.

As soon as Isaac entered the kitchen, Moses started meowing and walking around Isaac's feet. He was scrawny, with no food inside him. His voice was faint. His fur had lost its lustre. His cry of hunger failed to evoke any empathy in Isaac's heart. Even today, he was not at all bothered. He was furious with the rabbi. He put an egg on to boil. He would have an egg sandwich and some soup for his dinner. He was seething inside with rage like the water boiling in the pot. Moses still meowed as he walked around Isaac's heels. Suddenly, who knows what took over Isaac. He dipped a ladle in the pot, took some boiling water, and poured it all on Moses. Moses screeched, his cry sounding like the burning charcoal that had fallen on Isaac's hand and left its mark there forever.

Moses stood still for a while, his eyes blazing. He gazed into Isaac's eyes with his burning eyeballs. For a month he had been starved or half-fed. Moses had been like Miriam's own child. What happened next? Like a tiger that has just learnt to kill its prey, Moses pounced on Isaac Perring. He was faster than a storm and took Isaac by surprise. He was like a lightning bolt. He gripped Isaac's throat with all his might. His back was still hurting from the boiling water.

No matter how he tried, Isaac couldn't get Moses off his throat. Moses slit Isaac's windpipe and flung him down on the floor. Terrified, Isaac saw not Moses but Miriam's face in front of his eyes. He hallucinated for a few seconds. Before he could find out whether it was Moses or Miriam, Prophet Moses sent Isaac to the great beyond by tearing his windpipe. He still had his burnt back. Isaac was unable to get Moses to release his throat. From where this straved Moses got so much strength like prophet Moses hard to tell.

Now Moses reached heaven with his teeth still gripping Isaac's throat to explain his case. It is quite difficult to predict where Isaac would go leaving his business behind. But Moses would definitely go to heaven where Miriam waited to welcome him with a plate of GoCat and Whiskas, flavoured with love - "Moz moz my sweet cute boy!"

The people from the community completed Isaac's funeral rites. A person who lit just a single lamp to light his house year in and year out, whose business always ran at a loss, couldn't possibly have any money. His cupboards and drawers were empty. No passbook from a building society, no deposit book, no cheque book in any of the drawers. The rabbi felt guilty, thinking that he had unnecessarily tried to get money out of someone who didn't have any.

A few of Isaac's relations came from Israel to auction the house along with all his belongings. The rabbi was happy to finally get some contribution. Everything else in the house was auctioned. All his old furniture and the like. A newly married couple, who were builders by profession, bought the house. They planned to renovate the house to their liking.

The couple worked till they almost broke their backs.

One day, the builder whispered to his wife, "Julie, I think Isaac hid something under the wooden floorboards. Who knows whether it is the body of someone he killed?"'

The couple removed the floorboards. They had not yet done anything to the floor of this room. After they had removed just two boards, they saw something hidden underneath. They both felt a bit nervous when they saw a black boxlike object. They had found some invoices and an adding machine in the room. After removing the floorboards, they did not find a rotting corpse but some wooden boxes. The boxes were hidden behind the black box. They opened the boxes and screamed, their hands covering their mouths in astonishment, "O dear God, O sweet Jesus!"

They almost had heart attacks seeing the money in front of their eyes. Stacks and stacks of money. Fifty-pounds notes, ten-pound notes, five-pound notes, hundred-pound notes and some five-pound coins. There were some boxes just of coins. Ali Baba's hidden treasure under Isaac Perring's floorboards! They could not finish counting all the money that night. Isaac had not written a will about what was to be done with the money. Perhaps he had not thought that he would die so soon. He might have lived for another twenty years. He would have hoarded more money under the floorboards of the dimly lit house. Another wooden box would have been added. He had been given a piece of burning coal instead of a piece of bread when he was young and had caught a terrible disease named "hoarding." Moses might have called the disease something else.

Isaac used to think of Moses sometimes as Hess, sometimes as Mengele, sometimes as Goering. Moses didn't prove him wrong. Moses didn't prove his thoughts of Miriam wrong either. He had only survived for the past one month because he could smell Miriam. Both he and Isaac Perring would have been alive if he could have had only one-tenth of a can of Whiskas. It would have cost Isaac Perring only forty-five pence. Miriam was not aware of the wealth below her floorboards. And Isaac never knew all the wealth Miriam kept in her heart. The way Bathsheba, Ruth, and Moses had known.

But then, not knowing about that wealth hidden in Miriam's heart and under the floorboards hadn't harmed anyone. Had it?

Translated by Niaz Zaman and Jackie Kabir

Mr. Brown's Feeling of Loneliness

Mr. William Brown is a quiet type of man. He speaks rarely and reads all the time. He is an omnivorous reader. He even reads every packet label and all the literature that comes with medicines. He has one hobby – fishing. He always chooses a quiet spot and spends hours there. He has a collapsible chair, different types of fishing rods, hats and flasks for tea, as well as books and magazines to spend long periods of time. He knows lots of fishing spots. He buys tickets to spend time there uninterrupted. He works now and again, but, most of the time, he is unemployed. When any fish swallows his bait and gets hooked, he whispers to it, "My dear, go back into the water. If I want to eat fish, there are fishmongers to go to."

Just sitting there in a place like that is his joy, and catching fish to free them again is also another joy. The fish look at him before going back into the water and disappearing. And he feels good.

He is forty-nine now. When he was young, one or two girls had tried to enter into his private life, but they found him boring, dull, and reserved. He never liked to dance all night, make love for a long period of time. And using sugar-coated words for them was not his style. So a number of girls had come but within a few days vanished. Living alone is his choice and he feels good. He loves books, fishing, and occasionally a holiday in a place which is quiet and has fishing opportunities.

But something happened which changed his life. That something was, oneday, in the Unemployment Benefit Office, for no apparent reason whatsoever, a girl was staring at him. He was reading a book sitting in a corner. For him a classic was good enough to kill boredom or pass time. The girl was Rosemary – a girl of mixed race. Her mother was English and her father Jamaican. She had lots of wild curly hair and huge hazel eyes, a kind of olive complexion and a buxom body. For whatever reason, Rosemary felt something for him and followed him home. Her heart felt a kind of tingling pain for this quiet man. Who can explain why in this world now and again unexpected or odd things happen? After that, a series of incidents took place, and, with a few guests, they got married in the church. It was a first marriage for both of them. He had never been married and, though Rosemary had had a number of boyfriends, she had never been married either. What she saw in him when he was reading a book or drinking tea from his flask was not clear. Could it be Mr. Brown's new shirt or his new haircut? Who can tell?

After their marriage, Rosemary tried to control everything – his life, his purse, his books, his hobbies. Mr. Brown realised marriage was not for him and tried his best to slip off the hook just like a fish which has swallowed a bait. But Rosemary was reluctant to let him go that easily.

Like a stern guardian, she tried to control everything and his every move. Like a dictator she told him, "You must not read those books, Wills. Read some romantic books by Jackie Collins or Barbara Cartland or someone else. Stop reading classics."

"Do not spend so much money on fishing, rods, baits, tickets."

"Do not listen to all that Beethoven, Mozart, Bach, and Handel. Listen to some easylistening ones."

"Do not wear those shirts and trousers. Wear something smarter. Why do you want to look so old all the time?"

"And why do you make love so quickly? Have those pills and potions and be virile." She got all sorts of aids for him, but he was reluctant to use any.

On their first marriage anniversary, the two went to a nice hotel – it was Rosemary's idea. But the frustrated Rosemary threw all her presents out of the window; she poured black ink on the bedsheets and clothes. Next morning, Mr. Brown escaped from his wife and went to Spain to live the rest of his life there. Once before, he had seen that fishing village and loved it. He preferred his independence to his little house and that farcical incident everybody calls marriage. He packed up his things and took all the hidden savings he had kept in the bank for rainy days.. The secret money that Rosemary did not know anything about. He sneaked out from the hotel in the middle of the night when Rosemary was fast asleep and from Rosemary's reign forever.

Rosemary came home alone. Maybe she was tired of trying to keep someone on a leash for a year. She just yawned.

Twenty years gone. Mr. Brown returns from Spain to find his house is not his, someone else is living there. Where is Rosemary? No one knows where she is. Is she dead or alive? No one can tell him about her whereabouts or her present address or how she is keeping. Has she gone to a different country? New Zealand, Australia, South America? No one can answer that question either. Then Mr. Brown stops thinking about her, feeling blissfully happy because she is not there anymore.

When he visits his house, the new resident tells him, "My father bought this house twenty years ago." Then the man slams the door shut angrily.

So Rosemary had sold the house as soon as she was single again. Mr. Brown thinks he has found the reason for her madness or love for him – a cute Victorian house! He mutters angrily, "Greedy cow!"

But only Rosemary could tell whether it was only the house or some feeling for the man who was sitting in a corner and drinking green tea from the flask while reading a classic – *Far from the Madding Crowd.*

Mr. Brown gets another tiny council flat. It is small but adequate for him. With his social security benefits, he is doing all right. He has a bit of savings too. He is seventy. He feels as happy as a lark, fishing, reading books, and being back in his own homeland with no such rubbish as Rosemary to control his every move. Why shouldn't he be happy? He talks to fish, trees, air, grass, and stars. The bottom line is that he talks to himself all the time. "My dear fish, go back into the water." Or when he sees a tree with some branches chopped off, he will say, "My God, who has chopped your hands and legs like that?" He caresses the tree as if it is his beloved friend and says, "You should be okay soon." He touches the tree as if he is touching someone with an amputated leg. And only he can hear the tree whispering back to him, "I am okay. Please do not worry about me." A silver birch or poplar makes him sad sometimes and then he returns home and sits down to read a book. Evening has its mystery. Under a floor lamp, he thinks differently. He can see the stars and the moon from his tiny balcony and through the window. The characters in the book are with him now. "You do not like the way the writer ends the story, isn't it? Do not worry. I will be in some other book and live there." "Listen now. I am Ruby. A

rich man's only daughter. I am not Doris anymore."
They talk to him in these mysterious moments.

Then he opens his eyes. No one there. No Ruby or
Doris. He closes his eyes again and thinks about all the
people in the books he has read. At one point he falls
fast asleep.

One day he is walking home quickly when he
notices a billboard in front of a funeral service. "If you
buy now, you can save up to 40 per cent." The shop
supplies everything needed for someone's funeral –
burial ground, coffin, headstone, wreath, flowers, a
Rolls Royce hearse to take the coffin to the graveyard,
etc. He thinks a little. Sometimes he gets chest pains.
Sometimes other pains. If I order or buy it now, I will
save some money. He is talking to himself again. Then
he enters the shop.

Two smart salesperson welcome him. One is a
man, the other a woman. The young man stands up
and says politely, "May I help you, sir?"

"Yes, you may. My question is, If I buy all those
things now which I need after my death and die later,
would those purchases be any good?"

"Yes, yes, of course. You write that in your will
and keep the receipt. We will honour it if you die even
after ten years. No problem with that, sir."

Mr. Brown sits on a chair and tells them the items
he wishes to buy.

"What sort of wood would you like for your coffin, sir?"

"I'd like mahogany."

"You'll get a mahogany coffin, then. But why don't you like oak or other wood, sir?"

"Mahogany has evergreen leaves and they look lovely."

The salesman is very quiet after that. A romantic man! He thinks.

Then Mr. Brown tells him about the headstone he wants. "Something like 'Here sleeps Mr. Brown/ A simple man no crown.''

The salesman takes notes.

Then Mr. Brown tells the salesperson about wreaths and the other items he wants. The salesman and the salesgirl take notes.

Mr. Brown smiles. "Do you know what I'd like? I'd like a few persons to turn up for my funeral service and drink on me to their hearts' fill."

"You must write what you wish in your will, sir."

"Of course, I will write everything."

After adding and subtracting, Sam the salesman says, "The normal price is five thousand but for you it would be three thousand five hundred."

"I will come back and give you the rest of the money. Now you can have fifty pounds as deposit."

"That would be fine, sir."

Then Mr. Brown asks, "I hope the pattern on the coffin will be fine and intricate. Will you make sure about that?"

"Please do not worry about those little things, sir. We make sure that the coffin looks immaculate and that one's last journey is something to remember. We have to think about your send-off thoughtfully. And also a place you can sleep happily forever. You know, sir, we know such place. Overhead lovely evergreen floral trees. Around you green grass and rose bushes everywhere. Yes, we know such place. Recently, we acquired a new cemetery. It was a park and now the authorities have made it into a cemetery. A lovely place for a final rest. It's called 'Lily of the Valley Meadow.' A real heavenly place, sir."

"Very good to know that." Mr. Brown tries to smile. Then he starts feeling rather thirsty and asks for a glass of water. He realises talking about death and all that can make people thirsty.

The saleswoman brings him a glass of water with two ice cubes.

Mr. Brown remembers something and says, "I remember a poem which I would love to have on my headstone – 'Do not go gentle into that good night.' It was written by Dylan Thomas. I love this poem."

"It is really a beautiful poem for a headstone. I know this poem. It's lovely." Sam the salesman smiles reassuringly.

At night Mr. Brown thinks about the purchases he has made. His cat, Nefertiti, cuddles next to him. He strokes her and says, "Nefertiti, when I go, someone will look after you. In my will I will leave some money for you, my darling. Please do not worry about a thing." Nefertiti looks at him, purrs, and then goes back to sleep again. Then he thinks about being alone and about loneliness for the first time in his life but does not know why.

Next day he looks out of the window and realises it's a nice spring morning. A summery sun welcomes him. He gets up and goes out for a walk. Those two again? Recently a newlywed couple has come to live next door. They walk like lovebirds, holding each other's hand and kissing and cuddling all the time. Mr. Brown looks at them, then he looks at something else. Another young man has wrapped his girlfriend inside his coat and the two are walking and giggling. He notices these scenes and starts feeling a kind of emptiness. God knows why he is feeling this emptiness or sadness? But it is absolutely true that this feeling is something new and out of character . He returns home soon.

For his lunch he finds a fish and chips shop. A rather good place to go. An elderly lady about his age is sitting alone at a table. No one is sitting in the chair in front of her.

"Hello," the lady says.

"Hello," he replies.

Then they start to talk. The quiet Mr. Brown feels chatty.

They talk and giggle like two teenagers. Soon the lady will go on a cruise with her friend Berty. They see each other often and spend time together though they live in different apartments. The lady with her lovely permed and dyed hair and red cardigan looks fabulous. A peacock brooch makes her cardigan even brighter. She also has a bubbly personality. After fish and chips, both of them have knickerbrocker glory – ice cream joy in a tall glass.

Mr. Brown is on the road again. The sky is bright and blue as if someone has cleaned it with Fairy liquid and J-cloth. He looks at the sky, then at the trees and finally at people. There they go again! Men and women, boys and girls, hand in hand, cheek to cheek, lip to lip. He is walking alone. Life is everywhere. He stares at a young couple who are running to catch the bus, hand in hand.

"Hello! Please be seated, sir," Sam the salesman gets up from his chair and welcomes Mr. Brown. Mr. Brown takes a chair and asks for a glass of water. The young salesgirl brings him a glass of water with two ice cubes. A minute ago Sam and the young salesgirl were doing something erotic standing by the wooden filing cabinet. In the shop of the dead something earthly. Now back to normal, they are alert and ready to please customers.

Mr. Brown coughs, clears his throat and says, "There is something you have to change for me. Would you write that please in my note of request?"

"Yes, sir, of course." Sam takes Mr. Brown's file out from the cabinet. Then he looks at Mr. Brown and waits.

"I'd like a big coffin."

The salesperson try to understand what Mr. Brown has meant by big coffin.

"A big coffin, like a double bed. Under a floral tree in the garden of the Lily of the Valley Meadow, surrounded by green grass and rose bushes, it would be very lonely up there on my own."

"Sir?" Sam tries to understand what does Mr. Brown want.

"A double coffin like a double bed," Mr. Brown mutters again.

Sam tries hard to think what the man actually wants. A double coffin like a double bed? Who is going to die with this lonely old man? Will both of them live or sleep in one coffin forever? Insane! He puts his pencil down and looks at Mr. Brown, bewildered.

One day, Rosemary was standing in a honeysuckle meadow and laughing her heart out at her boring husband's naughty jokes. Her wild curly hair was flowing in the wind as if a water nymph had come to the meadow to share a bit of time with him.

Last night this beautiful scene had kept him awake nearly all night. That was the first time he missed Rosemary. A woman with a huge appetite for life.

Sam is silent. He does not know what to say.

Mr. Brown asks for another glass of water with three ice cubes in it.

Translated By Saleha Chowdhury

Two lovers of Alisha and One more

Solaiman's poem is on the fax machine again! Alisha just got back from school. She notices it immediately. Another poem of love from him.

"Hey, you answer me. I love you from here to eternity. P.S Please do not go mad! It is just a poem."

Alisha takes the poem out of that fax machine. She tears it into pieces and throws it in the bin.

Three and a half years ago, Alisha lost her husband. She lives with her ten-year-old son Pial. She is thirty-one and looks lovely always Every body says she is glamorous. She has a lovely figure, and when she smiles, it is radiant. While her face is beautiful, her smile makes it even more beautiful. After her husband's death she hasn't worked. Although she still grieves, the boredom is getting to her, and she needs to work.

The man who wanted her for 24 hours a day is not there anymore. That man was Abu Karim, her beloved husband. He was also her best friend. In the emptiness of her life, she wants to find something to keep her busy. She saw an advert on a job notice board. *'Urgently needed - Classroom Assistant. Attractive salary and good prospect.'* She applied, and after a successful interview, she was offered the job.

Alisha met her friend Sujit in a conference. He was one of the three teachers who talked about the classroom assistant's job. Sujit Roy is from Kolkata. He is a scholar, and his biggest passion, is reading. He is a quiet man, and he rarely talks about his private life. He has strict moral principles, and others view his character as flawless.

They both live in Great Britain. During this time, Sujit has met many women. Some were, beautiful, some were alluring, while others were voluptuous. It seems he never entered a relationship with any of these women.

Now and again, Alisha hears Sujit's business like tap on her door. It's strange, but she can tell it's him by the rhythm of his tap. Whenever she hears the tapping, she wonders sometimes , 'has he ever dreamed of sharing a bed with anybody? Or has he already done that?' Alisha doesn't know. Although he talks openly on the phone to her, he never talks about his life before they met. When he texts her, his messages and emails reveal very little as well.

While they both like one another, and are the same age, they never talk about anything intimate. They never discuss human emotions, or their likes or dislikes, and for some reason, they prefer to keep things that way. The only intimate thing they know about one another is, Sujit was born in October, and Alisha birthday is in November.

While relaxing at home, Alisha thinks about the head teacher's compliments.

"You know Alisha, you can make a great teacher one day. If you don't mind, I will recommend you. You just need to complete your post graduate degree, and we can go from there. You can do it over two years. Evenings and weekends, or you can take one year leave of absence without pay. Can you afford that?"

While she had answered.

"Peter, please let me think about it, and I will get back to you."

At home, she is giving this a lot of thought. She has savings, and her husband left her some money. He also left the house she shares with Pial. And there is the lump sum from her husband's life Insurance policy. She can see that there are no financial obstacles, and she thinks, 'what should I do? What is the best thing? The Postgraduate degree will take a year. But a year is not a long time.'

The phone starts to ring. She is sitting in the dark and has forgotten to turn the light on. Through the doorway, she can see Pial in his room, he is doing his homework. She answers the phone and asks.

"Is that you Sujit?"

Sujit answers-

"Yes! How did you know it was me?"

Alisha giggles her response.

"Call it telepathy."

Sujit thinks about Alisha's answer, and he feels it is getting too intimate, and he changes the subject.

"Did you see the weather forecast. They say that tomorrow the weather will be horrible. According to the forecaster, there will be gale, blizzards and heavy snow."

Alisha recognises Sujit's emotional withdrawal, and she answers-

"Yes, I saw the forecast. Actually, I wanted to talk to you about something else."

Sujit asks-

"What do you want to talk about?"

Alisha answers-

"My head teacher Peter Mortimar spoke to me about doing a Post Graduate degree. He said, that if I complete this, then I can be a teacher. What do you think?

Sujit is delighted.

"Very good Alisha! It sounds like a golden opportunity. What are you thinking?"

While Alisha is happy at the way Sujit received the news, her answer is more cautious.

"I know teaching is a very demanding job. The idea of teaching for the rest of my life, feels exhausting. My Hasi Khala said, it's really tiring."

Sujit laughs.

"Okay, if not teaching, what else do you want to do?"

While this is his answer, he wonders, 'does she want to be a lady in leisure, or is she lonely? He doesn't ask this, instead he jokes.

"If teaching makes you tired, I am sure you can find another job. It won't be difficult for someone as glamorous as you."

Alisha answers-

"My reason for being a teacher is because of my son Pial. He is ten, and teaching will let me spend the holidays with him. I don't think other jobs will let me do this."

Sujit understands-

"Then why don't you work at a school until Pial leaves. After that, you can look at other options."

Alisha answers-

"By the time Pial leaves, I'll be an old lady!"

They both laugh, and with laughter in his voice, Sujit responds.

"I don't think so."

They then turn back to tomorrow's weather, and Sujit warns.

"I'd stay at home tomorrow. By the sound of things, it will be horrible."

Alisha is happy that Sujit is looking out for her, and answers.

"I will think about it. Thanks for your concern Sujit."

Sujit is smiling as he says.

"Not at all my dear Alisha."

After they both hang up, Alisha goes to Pial's room. She finds him making an origami boat. He is engrossed and doesn't notice her. Sitting next to him, Alisha asks.

"Pial, where did you get this origami book?"

Without looking away from the boat he is making, he answers.

"I got it yesterday. Uncle Solaiman gave me the book."

Alisha is confused and asks.

"Pial, which uncle?"

Still staring at the boat, Pial answers.

"Uncle Solaiman. You know him Ma. He has a shop, it's over there."

Then he points in the direction of the shop.

Alisha is quiet, but she is angry and thinks, 'love poems, phone calls and text messages, and now he is giving Pial gifts. Is it his way of getting close to me?' She supresses her anger, brushes Pial's hair, and asks.

"What else has Uncle Solaiman given you?"

Staring at the completed origami boat, Pial answers.

"Chocolates and crisps."

Alisha's voice becomes stern.

"Pial, I have told you not to take things from strangers."

Pial feels Alisha's anger, and he faces her.

"But Ma, he is Uncle Solaiman, he's not a stranger."

Staring back at Pial, Alisha answers.

"Pial he is not your uncle. He is not part of our family. Your real uncle lives in America, and we will be visiting him soon."

Pial find this hard and pleads.

"But Ma, he is really nice."

Alisha doesn't know what to say, but she can see that Pial is doing something good. Using the origami book, he's made a box, then a frog, and now a boat. He is doing all these things just by following the book. Also, he is having a lot of fun. She looks around Pial's room, and she see all the objects he has created. She smiles because they look so cute.

Pial tugs at Alisha's hand and asks in an excited voice.

"Ma! Look, it's finished. Do you like it? I know how to make three types of boats!"

Alisha smiles and asks-

"Are you making these all by yourself, or did Solaiman teach you how to make them?"

Pial answers-

"No Ma, he just gave me the book and some papers. I am following the instructions. See, steps 1 to 20. Sometimes there are more steps."

Again, Alisha smiles.

"My clever Pial!" She pats his back, and then she cuddles her son.

But when Alisha meets Solaiman at the shop, she is furious.

"Solaiman, please don't shower my son with your expensive presents!"

Solaiman is surprised at the outburst.

"Alisha, it was just a little book. It's not as if I gave Pial a car? Come on be reasonable."

Alisha is still angry, and it makes her voice falter. All she can say is-

"Still…"

And now Solaiman is angry.

"Alisha, do you take me for a stupid shopkeeper. I am not that. I have been to the University. I am a graduate, but I decided to do something independent. I have no boss. I have no one to tell me what to do, or when to do it. I am happy, and I am not short of money. Okay?"

Alisha knows she has been unfair, and now she clutches for something to give her anger some meaning.

"Why do you send me all these poems and love letters?"

Solaiman gives a reluctant smile.

"Alisha they are only poems. Where's the harm in that? Don't you like poetry?"

Alisha knows she is losing this argument, and she snaps.

"But you're wasting your time. I don't want them!"

Solaiman is calm, and there is no sign of anger on his face.

"I know that, but I think, one day, you will change your mind. I feel sure about that."

Alisha's answer is full of sarcasm.

"Really, are you?"

Alisha doesn't want to talk to him anymore. Some customers stare. While they don't understand what Alisha and Solaiman are saying in Urdu/hindi, they can tell by the tone of the voices, that it's an argument.

Seeing the looks on his customers faces, Solaiman's voice becomes gentle.

"Alisha, I believe you have a heart. And all I am doing, is trying to get close to your heart." Grabbing the moment Solaiman sings, *'Ek dilke tukre hajar hue.'* It means, my heart has broken into a thousand pieces.

Alisha glares at him.

"You are not a teenager. Stop acting like one!"

Solaiman, is stunned by her anger. Still remaining calm, he asks-

"Is sending poems only for teenagers? Alisha, are you just a teacher, or are you a woman as well?"

Alisha cannot supress her rage, and she doesn't care who is watching. She shouts.

"Go to hell!"

When Alisha is calm, she thinks, 'who can I talk to? They might think I am showing off. Because I have an admirer like Solaiman.' One thing she reluctantly recognises is, Solaiman is handsome and wealthy, and people like him, don't grow on trees.

Despite this, it doesn't feel right, and she isn't attracted by his wealth.

That night Alisha reads in bed. She has a book by her favourite author, Sunil Gangopadhay. She sees the title, 'Monishar dui Premik' it means 'Two lovers of Monisha.' It makes her laugh, but then she thinks about Sujit and Solaiman, 'but neither one is my lover.' She looks at the book cover, and thinks, 'Monisha's name sounds like mine.' With this thought she falls asleep, and while she sleeps, she has a smile on her face.

During the night, the sound of a severe storm wakes her. The noises are horrendous. She gets out of bed and looks out of the window. She sees lightening and then she hears the roar of thunder. It is a massive storm, and the wind pulls and pushes the trees in all directions. The creaking of the trees as they sway scares her, and she runs to Pial's room. Pial is awake. As soon as he sees Alisha, he runs into her arms, and she wraps her arms around him.

Alisha tries to soothe him.

"Pial don't worry, it will be over soon. I am here."

Holding onto Alisha, Pial answers.

"Ma it looks like a big giant is outside. It sounds like the giant is stomping about. The lightning is scary…"

When the thunder rumbles, Pial puts his hands over his ears.

Holding Pial tight, Alisha speaks in a whisper.

"You are right. I think the storm is a big giant and he is trying to scare everyone."

Holding Pial, she looks out of the window. She can see that the storm has wrecked the garden. She points at a tree and speaks.

"Look Pial, the tree has been uprooted. It looks like the giant is lying on the ground face down." Also, look at the garden, it is covered in snow."

With Pial holding her hand, she goes downstairs. She tries to open the door, but the pile of snow in front of it, stops her. She pushes with all her strength, but the door feels wedged shut. She'll have to wait for some of the snow to melt. She remembers Sujit's warning about the bad weather. They both go back upstairs, and sitting next to Pial on his bed, she speaks.

"You won't be able to go to school tomorrow. We will have to stay at home."

That pleases Pial, as he wants to make more origami statues. Smiling he speaks.

"Ma, tomorrow I am going to finish the whole book."

After a while Pial tries to go back to sleep, but Alisha senses that something is bothering him. Stroking his hair, she asks.

"Is everything okay?"

He opens his eyes and whispers.

"Ma you always help me when I'm frightened, but who helps you when you're scared?

Alisha smiles.

"I am alright, but what made you say that? Remember, I have you, and you can be brave for both of us."

Pial thinks about this, and then looking at Alisha he answers.

"But we haven't got a Daddy. I know that Daddy can make us feel good."

Alisha takes Abu Karim's picture from the shelf and puts it on Pial's bedside table. She stares at the photo. Abu Karim looks young and healthy. He has a tennis racket in his hand, and his smile appears eternal. Alisha feels encouraged and speaks.

"Look Pial, here is your daddy. You know something, he is always watching over us."

Pial turns his face away and gives a cold response.

"But it's just a picture Ma. It's not him."

Alisha goes back to her own room. She wonders, 'has Solaiman said something to Pial? Otherwise, why would he say such a thing.' She wants some advice, but she knows she can't discuss it with Pial. She speaks to herself, "I will handle it!"

In the morning Alisha phone rings, and it is Sujit. His voice is cheerful.

"How are you keeping Alisha?"

Alisha smiles and answers.

We are both alright, thanks Sujit."

Sujit asks.

"I know you are dedicated to your work, so I wondered if you tried to get to school?"

Smiling again, Alisha answers.

"I tried, but I couldn't get passed my front door. I must go in tomorrow. We have an important meeting. It's about the new syllabus."

Sujit becomes more serious.

"Take it easy Alisha. If the weather stays like this, your head teacher will have to cancel the meeting."

Alisha agrees, and adds.

"If he cancels, I'm sure he will phone, and let me know. I know Peter well. He will let everyone know if the meeting is still on."

Sujit accepts this and asks.

"Have you got everything you need?"

Alisha appreciates Sujit's concern and answers.

"Yes. Please don't worry. We are doing fine."

Sujit wants to help.

"I might come over and drop off some food. Just in case you are running low."

Alisha feels anxious, and answers.

"Sujit, please don't drive in these snowy conditions. It's slippery and the roads will be treacherous."

Sujit doesn't say anything, and Alisha knows he will try to visit.

During the day, Alisha and Pial make origami statues. After an hour, Pial loses interest, and goes off to watch television. Alisha tidies up, and then she starts to organise her files and folders. While she is doing this, she starts to hum a song. Pial hears her singing, and standing in the doorway, he speaks.

"Ma, I like your singing, it's very nice."

Pial's compliment makes Alisha smile.

"Do you really like my singing Pial?" He nods, and when he comes into the room, she gives him a big hug. In the middle of this, she hears the ping of the fax machine. She walks over to it, and she is angry and thinks, 'good lord! Even in this weather Solaiman is sending poems.'

This time the poetry is by Omar Khayyam. She sees the two Rubaiyat's.

Ah, make the most of what we yet may spend,
Before we too into the Dust descend.
Dust into Dust, and under Dust to lie
Sans Wine, sans Song, sans Singer, and--sans End!

The next one is.

Ah, fill the Cup. What boots it to repeat
How Time is slipping underneath our Feet:
Unborn Tomorrow, and dead Yesterday,
Why fret about them if Today be sweet!

Underneath the note he has written.
'Alisha, they are only Khayyam's. Please stay calm. Hope you two are keeping warm. I know you haven't gone to school today.'

Alisha decides to take Solaiman's advice, and she stays calm. She realises that her anger only encourages him to make these gestures. At first, she thought they were silly gestures, but she wonders, 'are they all silly?' She keeps this thought buried, but the feeling that something about this is not right.   She knows, Solaiman is not for her.

Eventually it stops snowing, and like a poached egg, a timid Sun tries to peep through the snow filled cloud. Looking out of the window, Alisha talks to herself, "I will go to school tomorrow, but Pial can stay at home. I'll call Usha to babysit." Usha is a student and has babysat before. Alisha pays her, but more than that she trusts her.

It is evening, and the Sun has set. Alisha hears a car outside her house, and slowly it comes to a stop. The business-like tap on the door tells Alisha that it's Sujit. He has brought food and drink. She struggles to open the door, and then she sees Sujit. She looks beyond him and notices that his car is standing in knee-deep snow.

She pretends to be angry.

"Why did you drive in this weather? Sujit, it's so dangerous, you could have skidded off the road."

He smiles.

"I didn't and I am safe. Anyway, this is a short visit. I need to get back, but here are some groceries."

Alisha returns the smile.

"Thanks Sujit. Please come in and have a cup of tea."

Handing the carrier bag to Alisha, he answers.

"No time for that. I must get back. It's getting dark and driving in the dark is dangerous. I better go."

He doesn't leave. Instead, he steps forward, looks into Alisha's big dark eyes. It is a long look. He touches her shoulder, and then he steps back. Alisha is quiet, there is gentle smile on her lips. Then Sujit leans a little closer and whispers.

"Don't worry about things. I'll always be around."

As Alisha stares at the car's headlight, she is deep in thought. She wonders, 'why would Sujit visit, if it is only to say, I will always be around. Why did he hide his emotion*s?* Why can he only talk about books with any real passion?'

Later another parcel arrives. It is from Solaiman, and his shop assistant delivers it. Inside, there are peas, soups, eggs, biscuits etc. There is a note attached. 'Please take these. It is just a gif*t*. Solaiman'

Alisha asks-

"How much do I owe you for the shopping?"

The shop assistant hesitates.

"Miss, I cannot accept any money. If you have a problem, you'll have to speak to my boss, Mr Khan.

Alisha has never been convinced of Solaiman's motives. To her, they are never what they seem. She would prefer to pay for these goods, but she doesn't want any drama, and after all it is not the shop assistant's fault. Turning to him, she simply says.

"Thanks."

Next day Usha is there to look after Pial. Alisha puts on her heavy coat, knee high boots, places her school bag over her shoulder, and heads for school. The meeting goes on for hours, and when it finally comes to an end, it is dark. Alisha stares into the darkness, and she sees that the snow has started to fall again. With care, she walks to the train station. Because of the snow, the trains are delayed, and many have been cancelled. After forty minutes, a train arrives, it is packed, and Alisha squeezes into the compartment. The train takes forever, and once she gets to her destination, she waits for a bus. She thinks about walking home. On a good day it only takes twenty minutes. But the snow is getting heavier, and the thought of walking in this weather is depressing her.

She needs the number 33 bus. It stops two minutes from her front door. But the bus is nowhere to be seen. She looks around, but there are no taxis, and the taxi rank is empty. She thinks, 'have all the taxi drivers taken the night off because of the shitty weather.' She knows she has no options. She'll have to walk.

Five minutes into her walk, a car slowly pulls up next to her. The passenger door swings open, and she makes out a face, but she doesn't recognise it. Then she hears an unfamiliar voice.

"Get in Miss."

Alisha is scared and asks.

"Who are you?" She's read about weirdo's who stalk the streets. Rapists, muggers, and thieves. She steps away from the car, she must know who this man is, before she accepts a lift.

The man answers.

"I am Ricardo Reis and I live in the next road to you. Your son Pial knows me. I taught him to ride his bike. Pial has a red bike. Please get in, otherwise please close the door. It's up to you Miss.

Alisha decides to take the lift. Not many people know about Pial's bike, and this makes up her mind. As soon as she shuts the door, she feels warm. The car has heated seat, and she feels the heat running up her back.

Once they start to drive, Ricardo speaks, but he doesn't take his eyes off the road.

"We are almost neighbours. You live in Daffodil street and I'm in Lotus close. From my window, I see you on most days, when you return from work. The bus stop is very close to my house.

Alisha asks-

"So, you know Pial well?"

Ricardo answers.

"I wouldn't say I know him well, but he is a bright boy. When you get home, tell him that Ricardo gave you a lift. I think he will be happy with that."

Ricardo is driving carefully, and the music is on. Alisha wonders, is it Mastroianni or Yanni? She doesn't know who the artist is, but the music soothes her.

Moving his head in Alisha's direction, Ricardo speaks.

"I am trying my best to avoid skidding. I hope you don't mind me driving so slowly."

Alisha smiles.

"Not at all."

Ricardo feels relaxed and starts to tell Alisha more.

"Thanks Alisha. You see in a fortnight I am going to Spain. It's would be bad if I were to have an accident. It might stop me from travelling."

Alisha asks-

"Are you going for a holiday?"

Ricardo answers.

"No, I am going to live there. This weather in England is not for me. I love the Sun, and a warmer climate. I have sold my house and I am ready to go.

Alisha asks-

"Are you taking all of your family with you?"

Ricardo answers-

"I don't have a family yet. My parents died about 5 years ago. I had a job, but I resigned. So, I have no family, and in a few weeks, I'll have no house and no job. As I said, I am ready to go."

Alisha wonders about, no family, and asks.

"What do you mean, you have no family?"

Ricardo laughs.

"Not yet. May be one day my Miss Right will come and pay me a visit."

He turns to Alisha and smiles. And in that split second, his gaze is deep. It stuns Alisha and she asks.

"What will you do when you get to Spain?"

With his eyes back on the road, he answers.

"I have bought a small two-bedroom house, and it is surrounded by lovely vineyard. I am going to produce wine, and one day, I hope to sell the wine."

He smiles again, Alisha smiles back at him, and Ricardo carries on.

"Small wineries can create great wines. They often produce fantastic products, like Vinsanto or a good Chardonnay. You don't have to be in Santorini or France to produce these things. If we take care of the soil and do some cross breeding, then…"

Ricardo stops.

"Sorry, I should ask. Do you know anything about wine?"

Alisha lets out a little laugh.

"Not really."

Ricardo grins and answers.

"You can learn, it's not difficult."

Alisha asks.

"How can I learn?"

Ricardo answers.

"Google it. You can get lots of information about wine, like top one hundred wines, most expensive wines, wine growing techniques, all sorts of things. It's interesting. Do you know which is the most expensive wine in the world?"

Alicia shakes her head, and answers.

"No, I have no idea."

Ricardo sucks in his cheeks with surprise, and answers

"Currently the most expensive wine in the world is a bottle of Domaine de la Romanee-Conti 1945. It sold at auction for £424,000, and a second bottle was sold at the same auction for £377,000."

Alisha is amazed.

"You're kidding. One bottle of wine sold for nearly half a million pounds!"

Ricardo laughs.

"It's true. Remarkable isn't it?"

Alisha agrees, and then she asks.

"Ricardo, do you drink a lot?"

He answers.

"I am almost a teetotaller. Producing wine will be my business. I won't be making it for myself. I let others do the drinking. But you know, Martin Luther, a German author and philosopher said, *"beer is made by men, wine by God."* I hope to produce wine of that quality.

Both Ricardo and Alisha laugh.

The roads are so bad, that the usual twenty-minute walk, or ten-minute drive has already taken an hour. Neither of them mind since they are enjoying the conversation. Alisha notices that Ricardo speaks with a soft tone, and his voice is gentle. He takes care, and he pays attention to each word he says. And after each sentence, he gives a reassuring smile.

They are at standstill. Ricardo looks across at Alisha.

"When I saw you from my window, I thought. You look smart and very independent. And the way you walk, suggests that you have carefree attitude. I notice Pial is like you, he is also Independent. I watched him, as he tried to learn how to ride his bike all by himself. When he saw me watching him, I think he realised that he needed help. I helped him, but I liked his confidence…"

Then Ricardo realises the traffic is moving again, and he changes the subject.

"Sorry, I can't go any faster. I hope it's alright with you?"

Ricardo is confused, and wonders, 'Am I driving slowly to avoid a crash, or am I enjoying Alisha's company.'

Alisha reassures him.

"It's okay with me."

Alisha isn't bothered how long the journey takes. She's already told Usha that she might be late, and she knows Usha will stay overnight if she must. Alisha doesn't mind if they reach home in the middle of the night, or the next morning. Ricardo carries on.

If I get bored with the wine business, I can do anything I want. I can work in the travel industry, but then I enjoy travelling. If I want, I can fix cars, build houses, work as a chef, or become a fisherman. What I am trying to say is, there are so many things we can do, if we put our minds to it. Some people call me a Jack of all trades, but I want to succeed in the wine business. Let's see If I can master that and produce some great wines."

Alisha sees something missing from the list, and while it has nothing to do with work, she asks.

"Ricardo, do you read books?"

Ricardo answers.

"I do. But just reading is not for me. I love life and you can't learn about life from a book, you must live life, and experience things. When I read, I often choose the classics. I am fond of classics.

Alisha smiles.

"Do you? I like the classics as well."

He smiles, and It charms Alisha, and she gazes at Ricardo, and her gaze is long and deep.

They pull up outside Ricardo's house, and he invites her in.

"Alisha, please come in for a few minutes. I have many classical books. I know I won't be able to take all of them with me. Take your pick and take them with you."

Alisha follows him. His home is cosy and warm. There is a log fire waiting to be lit. The central heating has been on for a while, and the heat from radiators make the house very comfortable. Alisha is looking at the log-fire. She wants to see the flames, and she wants the embers to glow.

Alisha was there not for a few minutes but for quiet sometime. Probably for three hours or so.

Sujit phone calls stop being answered. He doesn't know where Alisha has gone. It's as if she has vanished from the face of the Earth. Solaiman understands that all his poems and gifts are not enough to get close to Alisha's heart. But he isn't too heartbroken and starts to pursue a new love interest.

The house is close to the sea. Nearby there is a school for Pial, and about fifteen minutes' drive inland, is the vineyard. Alisha has found a job. She will teach English to Spanish children. Pial is enjoying life, and he loves the new and energetic father figure in his life. A father who is not just an image in a photo, but a three-dimensional character. Full of life and laughter.

Alisha sits in the courtyard, and there is a northerly wind around her. She sips on homemade Vinsanto, and then she looks at the crystal decanter that holds the wine. The decanter is on a table under a lush green apple tree. Alisha thinks about the latest entry in her diary and recalls her words.

'What else could I do? His smile made my heart melt, and his hand in mine felt like the warmest thing in the world. It felt like sunshine around me. How can any woman resist that?'

Translated by Saleha Chowdhury

Mira Sayal's Rose Garden

Mira Sayal was working in the garden. She was plucking the weeds and storing in a bin bag. Tomorrow is Thursday, the binman from the council is supposed to come to pick the bins. The blue bin is for the recyclable glass, paper and plastic, while the green bin was for food, garden leaves, weeds or grass. The black bin was there for the other garbage items. She was having a backache while plucking weeds by stooping low over the ground. She stood up straight for a while and stretched her back. She raised her hands and stood on her toes for a bit. Then, she looked at the roses. Many rose plants were there.Some of them were old, while some were newly planted. She had bought the tubs from the nursery and placed them here. The sky was clear. It would not rain today. But, can you really trust London's weather?

"Barkha, could you take to me Daisy-Dahlia Nursery please'' Her daughter listened to her. She lived in a small flat on her own and works in an office. Still she took her mother to Daisy-Dahlia Nursery one day. On that day, Mira Sayal had bought two sacks of fertilised soil, a big miracle grow and two new rose plants. On their way back, both of them had icecreams. They chatted like two old friends for a while. That miracle of fertilized soil and miraclegrow were now shining brightly in her garden. Mira felt great whenever sat on a chair and looked around at the flowers. The leaves were playing by themselves. A wonderful sight indeed! Her son Abinash had asked, "What would you like to have for your birthday ma?"

Pensioner Mira Sayal replied like a child, "A few chairs and a big umbrella over there for me baba!" To make her happy, son brought two chairs, a table, and a big umbrella with red flower prints. The happiness of getting these gifts brought tears to Mira's eyes. Now, she sat on the chair alone as her husband could not move much after having a major stroke. He had roamed around in the garden once or twice, but he could not sit here for long for backache. Mira sat in the garden with a two-band radio. She had either a sewing frame or a book with her. She liked the melody of tunes played by the classic FM station. Even though she did not know about musical notations, but she did not have any trouble enjoying music. It is very soothing. Her daughter bought her three solar lights worth 10 pounds. At night, the light glowed softly. Mira listened to the music in that soft glow and felt that there is no one as happy as her in the entire London city. Classic FM was playing something that made her tearful. At times, it made her happy and her heart flutter like a butterfly. Mira was alone in the rose garden. She had never thought of being happy with someone else in the garden. Although the moon was up, could it even illuminate London? Moonlight had been in exile long ago. But she did not even long for that moonlight when the solar light was on. The solar light seemed to enlighten the area. Her neighbour's garden had a solar lamp as well. Mira looked at that garden. Nope! it did not have much care. Only some apple and cherry trees. No one thought about flowers in that garden. An old lady lived there alone. Tormented with backache, knee pain, she did not have time for gardening. This eighty-year-old neighbour named Rosemary had been living alone for many years. A nurse came to see her twice a week, shopped for her, fed her medicines and helped her to have shower. There were many Rosemaries in Britain, who lived all alone. Maybe one day, she would either go to the old homes or float dead in the bathtub. Then someone would discover her dead body. After that someone new would buy the house and make a big garden. Mira looked at the red rose plant and said- "Barkha, see how many flowers the plant has now". Her rose plants had names, Barkha, Shanta, Hariyali, Abinash, Tinni, Anandi and many other names like these. And the plant that bloomed only yellow roses, Mira named it Asad. Who's name was that? Mira Sayal smiled to herself. There was a young man named Asad in their neighbouring house. The name Asad was given after him. Mira had not seen that face for the last fifty years or more. But still she remembered him. The lovely young man who used to play a mouth organ and juggled oranges or rubber balls with his hands. If he did not find anything, he used to juggle with tomatoes and potatoes. She still remembered him, and is there any special reason for it? Mira Sayal smiled on her own. A sixty seven year-old face lighted up with a smile..

She had put a black wig on her own hair. Most of her hairs had fallen out. She did not feel good to see herself in the mirror. That's why, a few years back, she went to the shop stealthily to buy a bob cut wig. Now, no one rememdered her real look with less hair. Barkha had bought another wig from Malta. That can be used with a bun. She used that bun wig whenever she wore a saree to attend a party. Some people wondered why her hair was short one day, and with bun other day. Eventually they knew the truth and no one asked any more question about it. And oneday Mira sharply told a nosey woman -"stop asking questions about my hair." There were many Mira Sayals like her, who wore wigs or hairpiece at an old age.

Haridas Sayal was at the door-"Mira, your phone".

Barkha maybe! Thought Mira. She wiped her hands and entered the room

"Who's speaking please?"

"I'm Shudha."

"Shudha?"

" Yes. A few days back, we've met on the bus, isn't it? I am that Shudha. Shudha Patel."

Mira Sayal remembered her. "So, what's up Sudha?"

"You'd told me that you were looking for green rose for your garden. Found that! Yesterday, I went to the nursery and found green roses. I've brought one for you, the rose is in the tub. Me and my daughter Padma found the plant. She bought one for her garden and I bought one for you."

"Green? I have red, white, pink, yellow, but not the green rose."

Shudha replied, "Redish-green. Not the stark green. Mira, I think you know that different colour of roses have different meanings, right?"

"What type of meaning?" Mira preteneded not to know the meanings and let her talk.

"Red means passion or love. White is for purity or sacredness. Pink is for love and tenderness. And the yellow one is the symbol of love that has ended. Or you can say, a symbol of being separated."

"What about the redish-green rose?"

"It means Celebration of life." Shudha gave her a hearty laugh.

Both of them had worked in a shop for a while. Shudha Patel from Gujarat. Shudha was a very ordinary person, not a daughter of a senior police office as Mira Sayal. Maybe her father used to be a farmer and she was married to an ordinary man as well. Her husband was not a technician as Mira's. He perhaps worked in a leather coat factory. Mira was not sure if he still worked there. Mira was now a retired clerical office of the civil service. She had met Shudha while doing an odd job in a shop.

Shudha was now 67 years old. She looked the same as before. Only her pain of arthritis increased. The feet looked swollen. She was wearing a saree with big green flowery pattern, like most of the other girls of Gujarat, Probably they were from the same area. Some of these girls had tattoos on their hands and legs. Shudha had a tattoo on her palm. When she met her on the bus, she sat beside her and chatted. There was no showingoff in Mira's behaviour or speech. A very simple Mira Sayal. She herself had forgotten that she had completed her M.A. in Urdu Literature. Even though the degree was of no use in Britain, there was always a literature and music lover inside her. She liked to listen to classic FM , buy records, roam around book shops and often returned home after selecting books from the library. Her choices did not match with Shudha. Still, when they met on the bus or street, they talked about pension, blood pressure, diabetes or their kids. The thought of Shudha bringing a rare rose plants made Mira very happy. Redish-green rose which is also the celebration of life! The symbol of life. Shudha told her about the plant in such a way that Mira began to think about a name already.

"Who was on the phone?" Haridas asked while watching T.V.

"You don't know her." Mira went back to the garden again. She didn't approve of this nature of Haridas. He wanted to know about the 14th generations of any person on the phone. Well, she never worried about Haridas' phone calls? Maybe, staying imprisoned at home had made him like this. "But anyway, there is no use in thinking all these."

While weeding, she brought a mug of tea and sat under the umbrella. The scorching summer light was covered with a shadow of clouds. The sun had hidden itself. She was enjoying the time, it seemed that the soft cloud with sudden rain will come anytime. Barkha was full of white flowers. Abinash was shining bright with red roses. Bindia had pink flowers and Asad bloomed a very big yellow rose. The Asad who juggled with oranges. They had live as neighbours for four years in Dehradun. Thirteen, fourteen, fifteen, and just when she was sixteen, they were transferred to Bombay. Her father was a senior police officer. After that, she had never met Asad. Now, she named a rose plant after Asad. Why? Who could tell why. Yellow is the symbol of "Goodbye Forever", the last meeting or the end of a relationship. Barkha kept on telling these things to her. Maybe Barkha was in love with a white guy. She never shared all these in detail with her mother Mira. In the same way, Mira was unaware of the trouble that Abinash was having with his partner, a Welsh girl. A black bird perched on the wall. Sometimes birds like this would come to the garden. Two apple trees were standing there side by side, first they filled with bossoms, and then they became small apples. Mira did not think much about the apple tree. She used to think more about the roses.

It seemed that she had started to read Mirza Ghalib's poetry after a long time. All these years, she was busy with office and did not have time to read all this. But now retired, Ghalid, Hafiz, Jalal Uddin Rumi, Fayaz Ahmed had returned to her life now. She did not write any literary work, but she had a passion for literature and also roses. Along with that she admired some western literature.

She put all the rubbish gathered in a corner into the big bin. Then she would throw them into the bin outside. Mira Sayal had turned 67 on 5th March this year. That's the time when she got the umbrella, table, two chairs and three solar lights as gifts. Horidas had crossed 74 and stepped into 75. He could not move around much because of a cardiac arrest five years back. He did not talk much either. But he sometimes went extreme with his investigations on what Mira was doing, with whom she was talking to.

Mira Sayal panned rotis for Haridas and some vegetables from last night with some curd. She had some tomato soup and a slice of bread She had taken off the homely clothes and put on a good Salwar Kameez. Also, she did not forget to take an umbrella with her. One could not really rely on the weather of the London. It was sunny now, and then it suddenly it started to rain. Sometimes it was freezing cold. And then hot and sunny. In London no one could keep up with the weather. She had a book in her bag to return it to the library. She liked the book by Anita Desai. Still now, Desai did not get the Booker Prize. But she deserved it, thought Mira. Today she did not issue any new book.

Shudha lived in Griffin road. It was 15 minutes by bus or on foot 30 minutes. Mira Sayal loved walking. She chose a short-cut to Shudha's, In due time she reached No 36. Griffin Road. It was Shudha's own house. None of Shudha's sons or daughters lived with her. Mira had never come to this house before. Today, she arrived to collect the green rose plant. Mira rang the door- bell- Ding Dong! The door was opened by someone else. That means Shudha had a tenant in her house. Mira would never do that. She would never rent her rooms to a stranger. Never. She did not like anyone else to interfere with the freedom she had inside the house. Her daughter Barkha came once or twice a week to stay with her. Abinash's did not stay with her. One of the rooms had books and it was her favourite room. When Abinash came, he preferred to stay in the room next to the living room, downstairs. There was no bathroom upstairs, and for that he stayed downstairs.

Shudha came forward to welcome Mira with a big smile. She took her to the small living room. Mira sat on a faded sofa. The vase on the table had paper flowers. There was a picture of Ma Santoshi on the wall. The other wall had the picture of a religious figure. It was Honuman or the monkey God. Another wall had the photo of Sai Baba, Shudha brought the tub. "Oh My!"- two redish-green roses had bloomed. There were three more buds in that plant. Mira hugged

Shudha ecstatically and said-"Thank you so, so much Shudha". Shudha did not take the cost of the plant and said-"You don't have to pay me." Mira insisted on taking the amount, but Shudha did not listen to her. After a while, Shudha brought Bhujia and tea on a tray and offered to Mira, "Please". Bhujia was homemade. Shudha had arthritic pain in her leg. She plopped her feet while walking. "Mira, you don't work anymore now, right?"

"No, I don't work. But there are so many things to do at home. You know I am really busy"

Shudha's husband was not at home. He did not have to go to work today and went to the doctor. He had chest pain and a weak heart. Informed Shudha, "He is not well. What can the doctors do? Alcohol and cigarettes have damaged his lungs and heart." After the long story of her husband's illness, Shudha changed the topic. Both of them reminisced the days of the cloth store where they worked together. Shudha enjoyed talking about those memories. They used to work together in the same shop, and then Mira had the government civil servant job. She had to attend an examination for it. And Sudha started to work as a factory worker in Charlton.

Shudha gets 500 pound every month by giving a part of her house on rent. She said Mira, "There are only two of you in the house. Why don't you give one of your rooms on rent? You will get about the same amount I get. As Greenwich University is near this area, many of the students look for places to stay." Mira replied, "My son and daughter come and stay with me sometimes. I should not give the room on rent." The house had her own study room, a lot of books, maybe Shudha would not understand all of these. Mira did not proceed with the talk about "renting room" anymore. Shudha had not studied much. Even after staying in this country for 40 years, she had a hard time speaking in English. Shudha was pretty different than Mira. Still, she was very happy because of the this rose. She invited Shudha- "Please do drop by my place someday, Shudha. I'll show you my rose garden." Shudha replied- "Of course, why not? I'll definitely come." Mira took leave from Shudha and came back home.Shudha reassured standing on the door -"Soon I pay you a visit."

Horidas was sleeping. The television was still on. Mira turned it off. Then she went to her garden. It was cloudy now, a drop or two were falling from the sky. Mira thought of potting the plant right away. In between Asad and Bindia. She dug the soil with a shovel and put a layer of fertilised soil. Then she took the plant out of the tub and placed it in the ground. Asad's yellow flower was shining brightly like a big moon. Bindia was her eldest sister's daughter who lived in New Jersey. Bindia was a bit dull, maybe in a few days, it will grow beautiful with the touch of Miracle Grow. Mira kept the tub with the rubbish. Now she would take all of the rubbish to the bin outside .The new redish-green rose plant was smiling in between Asad and Bindia. Mira looked at the colour of the new rose and wondered, "Can roses be so beautiful?" A few raindrops gathered on yellow Asad. The big petals of the flowers bathed in the raindrops and floated in the air. There was no big drops on Bindia.

Walking through the study room, spare bedroom, she would now go to her own bedroom. She would make a phone call or two . One of the calls would be to Bindia. How was she doing? Why her rose plant named Bindia looked so pale? Was there a connection between the two Bindias? Rose plant Bindia and real life Bindia? Was Bindia in any kind of trouble? A worry about Bindia was bugging her. She still remembered the day when 25 white roses bloomed on Barkha. On that day, Barkha got a good job. It happened in the last month, June. Today was July. May, June, July, August, September, October were the months when it bloomed to the brim. Then in Noember, the plants got trimmed for the next year. She usually remained busy in those days with sharp trimmer and sagitar. Now there would be flowers for the next four months. When the flowers would not be there, Mira would be feeling a bit sad. Then again, she would feel happy after a while and be busy with reading books and other works or probably jot down bits and pieces. Maybe she would go to the theatre or to national portrait gallery to look at pictures old and new. And stand in front of the portrait titled "The Poet". Mira did not know what was in that painting, but she could not remove her eyes from it. Many other paintings grabbed her attention. The thought of why she could not draw herself also came into her mind quite a few times. Though she was a student of literature, she could not write poems, or stories.. But sometimes she wrote a few pages' letters to the people who would appreciate them. Some literary flavours seemed in it and hidden emotions. . She often felt sad that in the era of mobile phone and emails, no one was interested in writing letters.

Mira now listened to the news from the two-band radio under the umbrella. Recession had affected the whole country badly. Only God knew what would happen. It was relieving for her to think that both Barkha and Abinash were still working. Her daughter looked after the accounts of an office and son remained busy with various responsibilities of a big firm. Both of them were self-sufficient, so there was nothing to worry about. The only difference was that none of them though about life as Mira did. They would not have house, garden, husband and kids in their lives. They would stay in the apartments and order take-aways. They would be busy with laptops and sports car and live together with someone but would not get married. If they did not like the person, they would break up. Having kids? That was a horror for them. None of them would like to get into the trouble of raising kids. Maybe that is the reason why the number of populations had started to decrease in Europe. What would she gain by thinking of these matters, son and daughter's future? Even if she thought about it, they would not change, their philosophy of life would not be different one. No question at all! But a mum's job to think those and Mira was not an exception. The moment she had entered the house with the two-band radio, she noticed that Haridas just woke up. It was his tea time with some biscuits. Or some fruit cake or fairy cake. Mira Sayal turned on the kettle of the kitchen.

Right on 2nd August , Shudha came to visit Mira's place. The garden was in full bloom. Two months had gone by. The apple tree had apples. Some of the them were hanging on the tree while Mira plucked some for apple *chutney*. After that, she had not plucked anymore. Bindia had large roses. Abinash did not have many flowers. A few days back, 13 flowers bloomed together on Abinash. Now it was standing quietly. No, Bindia did not have any bad news when the plant Bindia looked dull to her. Such changes in number and quality of the flowers did not bother her much. It was a misconception of her mind perhaps.

Shudha had called her before coming. Shudha's flower plant had six flowers and a bud She had named this plant Shudhamoyi. She liked having this rare plant in her garden. After receiving the plant, they had met only once. Shudha was running to the hospital for her husband then. He had gone through a big cardiac operation. What happened after that was not known to Mira. Here, people did not even know any news of next door neighbors, let one Shudha's news who lived in 30 minutes' walk away. Shudha did not say anything on phone, but her voice seemed gloomy. Mira also did not ask about her husband. Mira took a bit of special care of the plants because of Sudha. She sprayed some water on them and pulled out some leaves with the big broom. She cleaned the two chairs under the umbrella. She was coming around 4 o'clock in the afternoon. Now the day had become shorter. Everyone's opinion - It was an Indian Summer.

Apples were hanging in the apple tree. Horidas asked-"Who's coming?"

"Shudha, Shudha Patel. We used to work together, years back".

"Why is she coming?"

"Just to see me".

"She hadn't come all these years!"

Mira Sayal went to the kitchen. It was not necessary to answer every question. She fried some snacks. They could go to the garden and have them with tea.

Shuda arrived after 7pm. She was stuck with some important work. She was wearing a light blue dress with red flower prints. The waist coat over the dress had a peacock. Her hair was fluffed. She had thick hair and did not need any wig like Mira. But it looks less as she oiled it flat most of the time. Now her hair was shampooed and fluffed up. Shudha said-"This waistcoat belongs to my daughre Padma. She threw it away and I've picked it up to wear."

"Oh Really? That's why I was wondering, I haven't seen these before." Shudha's toes with red Kumkum marks were peeping from the two strings of her sandals. Today, everything about Shudha was different. Asked Mira-"How's your husband Ghonosham Patel doing?"

"It around a month or so that he has been living in a care home."

"Oh, that's sad indeed"

"Daru and ciggies, I mean alcohol and cigarettes. I'd shared with you earlier. All his life he was into these things. After we've bought the house, I have given it on rent. It was tough when our kids lived with us . Now they have left and are on their own. They are the ones to put him in the home. He needs 24/7 care now. His pension goes to the expense of the home. "

"How long has he been sick?"

"He was sick off and on for twenty years now." Shudha looked at the gardent. "Oh my! Isn't that my rose plant? The greenish red rose Padma had selected. Wow! It has flowers as well!" She went near the rose plant. Ghonosham would last only for a month or so perhaps. But Shudha's appearance did not say anything like that. Everything about her was new. Her swollen legs had reduced a bit as well. Shudha looked at the flower plant. Mira informed her that the plant was named after her "Shudhamoyi." Shudha was pleased to know that.

The two women sat under the umbrella. Evening was settling in, the solar lamps of the garden lit up. Horidas did not have dinner before 10pm. Mira Sayal kept chatting freely with Shudha. She said to Shudha, "Ghonosham, I mean your husband's news made me sad."

"There's nothing to be sad about! He has tattered his own lungs with daru and ciggies. He damaged his heart. Has he ever thought of me?" Mira Sayal thought of Horidas. Was there any difference between Ghonosham and Horidas? Only his own diseases and food. But still, when she wrapped up everything and went upstairs, Horidas kissed once or twice on her cheeks. He said- "Goodnight. Sweet dreams Mira." Mira either read a book or listened to music in her room and fell asleep.

It was much late at night while Shudha and Mira talked to each other. The solar light was almost like the moonlight. That's why every garden has solar lamps nowadays. A very heartwarming tune was being played on the FM station. Shudha asked-"I've sponsored and brought him into this country."

"Him? Who?"

"Listen, Mira my *yaar*. Five years back, I met this guy in my country. He is around 50 or 52. He is a widower and has a son who lives abroad. I liked him at the first meeting. No daru or ciggie. A very good human being. I sponsored him here to stay with me." Shuda spreaded her hands like the peacock's feathers On her waistcoat. A peacocks under the clouds waiting to dance in rain.

"Life is very short."Sudha uttered.

"Will he live with you?"

"Who else will he stay with other than me? I brought him here to accompany me."

"Do you want to get married to him?"

"No. We will live together like Padma."

"What will other people say?

"People? Who cares?"

Mira Sayal looked at Shudha Patel's face with surprise. Is this the Shudha with the pictures of Ma Santoshi, Sai Baba and Hanuman on different walls? There was an amulet around her neck. She remembered that once at their office a Muslim colleague named Khairun had touched Shudha's lunch box. Shudha did not have her lunch that day. She told Mira, "Khairun has touched it. Now I can't have that lunch."

"Why not"- asked Mira.

" I abide by my religion"

That day, Mira did not give a long lecture to Shudha,
But she was very surprised why Shudha believed in
touchable and untouchables even after living in
London for so many years. Shudha used to take bath
before completing her morning *puja,* supplications
every morning. Shudha is someone who did not study
much and lived with all these superstitions.

"You see Mira, I was thinking about my life. What
did I get in my whole life? Nothing. After giving two
kids, Ghonosham didn't give me anything. I've earned
money all my life. It was the same in my country as
well. Moreover, he will pass away soon, there is no
way to hold him back. I'm planning ahead for my
remaining years. The life I always wanted.

Mira Sayal looked at the garden. Mira looked
at the big yellow rose that was still fresh on Asad
plant. The solar lights in plants seemed mysterious..
Barkhad did not have any flower. A light tune was
being play by the classic FM. Shudha continued, "Life
is somewhat enjoyable now. I've been in the country
for so long. Let me be like them for a while. Live
together! Why not!."

"If Khairun touches your lunch box now, will
you eat of that box? You won't throw it to the bin?"

"Hell no! That is something else.

"That means you won't eat?"

"Kabhi nehi, never. I am a Hindu."

"Oh!" Mira did not like her opinion. She said-
"You haven't changed much. Only—"

"I only know that I have to live. I want to live many more years to come. Pradip is a good man. He has a good physique." She raised her hands above her head as if she was hoping to touch the sky, and her body seemed to be very stout and youthful. She took out a mirror and put lipstick on. She retouched with her puff on the cheeks and said- "What you are thinking of me, I don't know. But I'm desperate. I love to live anyhow, not waiting to die and hoping to go to paradise. Ptodeep once told me - We live just once."

Mira Sayal did not say anything. She just said-"Maybe you are right Shudha. Sometimes we should think about what we really have in our whole lives."

"You're an educated woman, your situation is different. I used to work in a saw mill in my country. When I came here, I did various odd jobs to run my family. Sweeper, cleaner and what not. The job that I did with you was the best job I've ever had. Now I get pension, I ma 67 years old. Let's say and hope if I live ten more years or so, I want to live my life the way I like. Just for once I want to be really happy Mira. Is there any harm in it."

What could Mira say at this point? The woman whose husband was about to die soon, she had begun her life anew. What advice should she give her? Uff!

Why would she even do that? If Shudha did not want to be like her next door neighbour Rosemary, that was her own choice. It was her life - Mira realised it well and that is why did not want to advise her. or give a long lecture on morality. Just very softly uttered - "Have a happy and enjoyable life Sudha." Sudhas eyes seemed misty.

Shudha went away after a while. Horidas had his dinner. Mira Sayal looked at the garden from her window. The flowers of the garden could be seen. It was looking heavenly under the solar lamps. 13, 14, 15 and as she stepped into 16, they had to leave Dehradun. Asad Hashmi's father was a doctor. Asad was perhaps 20 then at best. That lovely young man who juggled oranges or balls with his hands. He used to play various tunes on his mouth organ. Mira Sayal was looking at the garden and thinking about him.

Asad was fighting for life in one of the Nursing homes in California. It was the last stage of cancer. His two wives have left him one after another. Many other women came into his life. But still he remembered Mira's face. Mira Malhotra. She used to look at his juggle with her huge eyes and open mouth. Long braided hair on her chest. 13, 14, 15 and the moment she stepped into 16, they had to leave Dehradun. She did not give the time for him to express a special feeling that he had for her. He would have said it to her either today or tomorrow. Then? Who knows what would have happened after that? If he somehow knew that a rose plant in Mira's back garden was named Asad, he would have been able to breathe his last with a strange happiness. But everyone was not that lucky in this world to know such a news. A rose plant named Asad was glowing in the garden. Mira could not forget him even now. If Asad Hasmi was 72 now, Mira was 67. But he remembered the school-going Mira with braids hair with red flowers. Pretty Mira who used to giggle in everything and opened her mouth wide with surprise to see him juggling. Her huge eyes were filled with Kajal. And a tiny Bindia.

Mira Sayal woke up in the morning. She had a habit of Pranayama. She would sit on the garden chair. In the winter, she sat inside the house and in summer, she preferred outside. She had fallen asleep while reading a book last night. Mira had dreamt a haphazard dream. Such a nuisance! Such a dream at her age? She saw that someone hugged her and was kissing her passionately for a long time. Shudha! She is the cause of such a dream, said Mira to herself. Her discussion on such topics brought all these dreams. Mira washed her face with soapy water well in the morning and came to the garden. She looked at the wall of the garden where different birds came to rest. A blackish-re bird was sitting on the wall. Redish feathers with white legs. It was a different one. Where did the bird come from? Previously, other types of the birds came to perch on the wall. During the last Eid day in Dehradun, Asad Hasmi had worn a gorgeous Punjabi. The colour of the punjabi was blackish-red, with some yellow needle work on the chest. The pyjama was white. Not really a *chost* pyjama, but somewhere between a *chost* and a lose pyjama. His body emitted fragrance of *attar.* He had *surma* on his eyes, dressed up for Eid. Mira looked at him mesmerised, "You're looking great. Really lovely."

"Really?" -said Asad. He played the tune of *Aye Mere Dil kehi our chal*-"My heart lets go somewhere else."- Then turning back a radiant smile for Mira.

The bird on the wall had redish-black chest with yellow spots here and there, white legs..

Translated by Sabreena Ahmed

Talking Their Hearts out

I got up late that morning and for no apparent reason I was still tired, and struggled to get out of bed. Looking through the window, I saw an icy town. There were some grey houses, and some colourful ones. Then I remembered something. It was the calendar. It was a special day, and an asterisk was telling me something. After a mug of black coffee and a slice of toast, I wanted to hear music, something nostalgic, some old Bengali songs. Sometimes I did this while I shaved, and carried on while I got dressed. I decided this is what I would do today.

Suddenly, my phone rang. When I answered, I heard a familiar voice.

"Hallo Sir! What are you doing?"

Smiling I answer- "Oh Jay, how are you, and why are re you phoning me?"

There was a pause, and then Jay answered.

"Sir, we have a meeting at NASA office, it is at ten o'clock. Do you remember"?

I nodded. -"Yes, I remember. Don't worry Jay I'll be there."

Jay's answer was less anxious. -"See you there Sir!"

-"See you Jay".

Joydeb, or Jay as we knew him, came from India. While we were together, he worked under my supervision. He was doing a postdoctoral research on supersonic technology. While Concorde was fast, it proved to be a horribly noisy aircraft, and no longer up to the mark. We were trying to improve this, and develop something better. We had many other projects, but aircraft development was the most important one.

Jay's work was great and thought provoking. I liked his choice of research subject, and often discussed aircraft concepts, and the development of supersonic technology. Since the discontinuation of Concorde for its inefficiency, we were trying our best to find alternatives. My own research was on noise reduction.

Jay told me - "I would love to do some works on rockets, since everybody believes NASA means rockets, or going to the moon. People think that at NASA, our lives are like something out of Star Trek."

Jay was clear why he liked rockets and astronauts. Maybe, that is what he wanted to do. Maybe it would allow him to show off.

When memories of my conversations with Jay passed, I remembered why the day was special. The meaning behind the asterisk came to me. It was the date of our language movement. It was 21st February. I looked at the calendar again. Perhaps my daughter Sophie put an asterisk on the calendar.

All of my family was scattered in different places, and I was alone. While I dressed, I heard an old Bengali song loud and clear, and it made me feel nostalgic.

My office was half an hour drive away. As a senior scientist, I had to be on time, since my boss expected that from me.

In my car, the music played. The road was icy, and so I drove carefully. Again, I thought about Jay. A brilliant young man from Kolkata, and he worked hard. He told me he enjoyed working with me. I was very pleased, because I had many research students work under my supervision, but none of them came from the Bengal.

I knew that in my office, there were scientists from all over the world. China, Japan, Australia, New Zealand, Egypt, and other places, but other than Jay, there were no Indians. We all spoke English, and all our research papers are also in English. It is amazing, that 21 consonants and 5 vowels make the world go round. What would we do without the English language? I looked at my watch, and I realised I was driving too slowly, and I put my foot on the accelerator.

As I drove, a song played, and it made me think about Mithukhala. It was a special song. Since it was a song, we both loved.

"I know how to solve the problem!"

Echoes of her voice raced through my mind. I remember the day Mithukhala told me how to solve Concorde's noise problem. I was excited and asked. "How?"

"Get a big silencer and fix it to the engine."

She was serious. I remember listening, and thinking, no she could not be serious! It sounds crazy. But sometimes that how she solved problems. I know she has a good heart, and corner of her heart is for me. I love to believe that.

At her idea of the silencer, I just said. -"Let me think about it".

We grew up together, and she was always a friend. She was a few years older than me. She wrote stories, read all sorts of books, and some of them were western. When she told me about the silencer to quieten Concorde's noisy engine, it seemed just like one of the stories she read. When she needed a bit of peace and quiet, I think these stories worked for her, and allowed her to escape. "And I have my own silencer too" .She told me once. "It is music." Now, her children have grown up, her husband has died, and she is on her own.

In the car, my phone starts to ring, and Mitukhala's name appears on the screen. It feels like telepathy. "Hi babu how are you? Today is 21st of Feb. Have you got anything special to celebrate?"

As usual, Mithukhala's voice is cheerful. I turned up the music so she can hear the song. It was Tagore at his best, and she was ecstatic. -"Are you listening to that song Babu? Bless you."

She laughed. -

Then I said "Yes' I am Mithukhala!"

But then the phone became silent and faded. A bad signal ended our call.

Once in my office, Jay and I had a long talk about astrodynamics. Jay was doing some blue prints for his thesis. I advised him, and he took some notes. It was always our conversation in English, and it was polished one without hesitation. During it, I said- "After work, I need to go to Algrave." It is a super market where I get my groceries.

He asked -"Sir, can I join you?'

I smiled, and answered. - "Of course, you can"

I had my lunch in the canteen, and again I saw Jay. We were both deep in our own thought. I was thinking about my work to address the underlying mechanics of various flow phenomena, which affect aeroplanes and pollutions. I was also thinking about "dynamic stall", and the impact a sudden gust of wind has on aeroplanes wings. I remember telling Mithukhala about this, and she said to me -"Camouflage the wings." As usual she replied like an eternal problem solver.

I was astonished, but I didn't ask her to explain. Instead, I thought, "camouflage the wings!" Are you joking?" The way she suggested was not joking at all. She was dead serious. That's how it did look though. And that was her style, always.

In this problemic world it seemed she always had a solution .

Looking over at Jay, I knew he would be happy to work on the rocket division. This is what everyone believes NASA does. We Travel to distant planets in rockets, and then return to the earth, with bits of soil or rocks.

After work, we drove to Algrave. Both of us parked our cars, and walked to the store. While walking, a sharp stone hit my leg. It was very painful, and I screamed in Bengali. "Mago ami gelam!"

It means, "Mother I am finished" and hearing this, Jay looked at me with panic in his eyes, as if he had just seen a ghost. As the pain subsided, I looked at Jay with surprise, and I wondered, what was it that made his eyes look like saucers?

With sheer amazement in his voice, Jay asked. "Are you Bengali?"

I answered. "Yes I am. Why do you ask? Didn't you know?"

He replied. "No, never, I thought you are from Egypt."

With a smile, I asked. "Egypt? None of my ancestors or my relatives comes from Egypt. Why did you think that?"

Jay hesitated. "You have a Muslim name, and you hold such a senior post".

I asked. "Senior post? Do you think Bengali's cannot hold this post?"

Again, he hesitated. "Not exactly but ---"

Finding his words, Jay said. "Dada let us sit down on that bench"

We sat on the bench and spoke for over two hours in Bengali. Again, Jay was surprised that I was from Bangladesh and not from West Bengal.

We spoke about the geographical divide of Bengal. We wondered if it was a legacy of the British policy to divide and rule. We spoke about The Punjab, our fathers, our siblings and our history. We talked about Mum's cooking lentils, fish, bari, saag, and all of these things came to life. It felt like every subject brought back a vivid memory, and gave our conversation a new dimension.

From that day, I became Jay's Dada, and he was my younger brother. He never called me Dada in the office. It was always a private greeting.

When we sat together, or spoke on the phone, Jay would laugh a hearty laugh, and say- "Dada it is so good to talk in our mother tongue. It takes me back, and I remember everything."

About twelve o'clock at night Mithukhala's phone rang -'Hi Babu have you enjoyed the day? How did you celebrate your 21st among all those robots like scientist? God! they never smile " I replied "Mithukhala -You would not believe what has happened today. You might think I am just making it up like old days-- "

"What was it Babu?"

"Very special something. It was a splendid experi---"

The line got cutoff . I could not finish it. The bad line again ended our call.

For me, that was the best 21st February celebration I had in a very long time. Who would have thought it? During our two-hour conversation, I always remember there was a special subject, and that was our language movement. Towards the end of the conversation, Jay looked into my eyes, squeezed my hand, and said. "Dada we are all so proud of you!"

He said it as if I was Salam or Barkat, or I had just got back from my fight. Was I tearful? I do not remember it now. Whenever Jay and I talk, we remember our country, our language, and walking by a flowing river. We also remember our roots, history, and traditions.

Just talking can be so refreshing!

Translated by Saleha Chowdhury

Printed in Great Britain
by Amazon

82837019R00149